NIGEL WATTS

Nigel Watts was born in Winchester in 1957. He has travelled widely throughout Asia, spending two years in Japan. He is a trained teacher and a professionally qualified shiatsu therapist. His first novel, THE LIFE GAME, won the 1989 Betty Trask Award for best first novel, and is also published by Sceptre. BILLY BAYSWATER is his second novel.

Nigel Watts

BILLY BAYSWATER

sceptre

Copyright © Nigel Watts 1990

First published in Great Britain in 1990 by Hodder and Stoughton Ltd.

Sceptre edition 1990

Sceptre is an imprint of Hodder and Stoughton Paperbacks, a division of Hodder and Stoughton Ltd.

British Library C.I.P.

Watts, Nigel
  Billy Bayswater.
  I. Title
  823'.914[F]

  ISBN 0-340-54476-7

Printed and bound in Great Britain for Hodder and Stoughton Paperbacks, a division of Hodder and Stoughton Ltd., Mill Road, Dunton Green, Sevenoaks, Kent TN13 2YA. (Editorial Office: 47 Bedford Square, London WC1B 3DP) by Clays Ltd., St Ives plc.

To Sue and Nichola,
darling sister, darling niece

Billy's got summat wrong with his brain – that's what they say. I touch my face in the mirror and smile. Billy Bayswater brain.

I wrap the scarf tight round my neck and pull on my coat. It's blummin cold today. Real winter weather now. Let's hope Mr Fred'll share a cup of coffee with me in the hut. That's the best bit of the day, when Mr Fred and me drink coffee with the rest of them on the building site. I like Mr Fred – he's got a good smell from his pipe, and a red thermos.

I look up and down my body to check I'm all ready. Coat – I shake the pocket. Money. Boots. I feel my head – hat. Gloves. Ready.

I have a last look round the room and sort of say goodbye to the plants. They don't grow much in winter. It's too cold I suppose. They don't really like the cold, that's why they sort of go to sleep I suppose. Someone told me plants make the air. It's hard to figure that one out – but they *do* smell good. Sort of green and cold and wet.

Mr McDonald's in the hall. He's dressed in his smart mac, but he's still got his slippers on. I stare at them.

'Gout, Billy. You know what that is?'

I shake my head.

'Well, let's hope to God you never do.'

He sort of shuffles to the door and I dart in front of him to open it.

'I hope you feel better soon, sir.'

He gives me a nod and then goes down the steps to the road. A man's waiting for him in his car. It's Mr McDonald's friend. I know cos he's there every morning to take Mr McDonald to his work. I dunno what job Mr McDonald does – I think he works in an office or summat, cos sometimes he comes home with a briefcase and that. His friend's reading a newspaper. I see the car most mornings, but somehow it looks specially nice this morning. It's sort of maroon, like one of them big soft plums you can buy. I run my fingers over the bonnet. It's all sort of frosty and there's a mark where my fingers've been.

'Nice car, sir.'

Mr McDonald sort of smiles at me and half gets into the car. His feet are hurting him. I can tell by the way he looks all sort of tight. I suppose it's that thing he told me about. His friend's still reading the paper.

'Do you remember how to get to work, Billy?'

I give him a nod. 'Down to the letter box and then past the flowers and just before the tables I go this way – '

I point. I've been working on the building site for ages now – I can remember easy how to get there. I used to get lost at first, but now I don't. I know the way real good.

Mr McDonald gets into the car and slams the door.

'Cold today, Mr McDonald,' I say, but he don't hear me. I sort of stand there watching them. It's real nice, this car. Sort of like a plum.

Mr McDonald's friend puts the paper down and says summat to him. He's smoking a fag – there's half an inch of ash hanging off the end. I hold my breath waiting to see if it's going to fall off. It does, just as his friend folds up the paper, and I let out my breath. I watch the car drive off, and breathe in the exhausty smell it leaves behind.

I want to dance, but I know I shouldn't.

*

Mr Jarvis the foreman's in his hut. He's leaning over a table looking at some plans. He don't see me at first cos he's so busy reading and that. There's a mug of coffee on the table, all hot and steamy. Normally I make his coffee. I know how to do that – two spoons of sugar and the top of the milk – but someone else's made it this morning. Usually it's my job – it's what I do first thing I get to work, but now someone else's done it.

I stand there by the table, and he looks up after a bit.

'What the hell are you doing here?'

He's surprised like, and I dunno what to say. 'I told you on Friday we won't need you any more.'

Mr Jarvis has cut himself shaving. There's a little V of dried blood by his ear.

'Billy, did you hear what I said?'

'Yes, sir.'

I wait a bit, pressing my finger against the edge of the table. Summat's wrong – I can see that. Mr Jarvis don't say nothing, he just looks at me.

'Can I make you some coffee, sir?'

Mr Jarvis pushes his cap back and sighs. He ain't pleased. I dunno why, but I can see he ain't happy with me. Maybe it's cos he had to make his own coffee or summat.

He leans over and bangs the door open with his fist.

'Fred! Come over here a sec.'

Fred's carrying his toolkit. Sometimes he lets me carry it, and it's real heavy. It's full of tools and that, and it weighs a ton. He comes in the hut and drops the bag on the floor. Then he looks at me.

'Oh hell, Billy. You're not supposed to be here.'

'Look, Fred,' Mr Jarvis says to him. 'Explain to him we've finished with the navvies. There's no work for him here.'

Mr Jarvis turns and speaks to me now. 'Don't you understand?'

He speaks like a foreigner or summat – one word at a time, slow and careful like. 'There's . . . no . . . more . . . work.'

His teeth are all crooked, and one of the top ones is grey and soft-looking like an avocado that's gone off.

Mr Fred squeezes me on the arm. I can smell pipe on his breath.

'Do you remember the cards we gave you on Friday? The little slip of paper?'

I take it out of my pocket. It's a bit creased so I smooth it out.

'That's the one. Now, look. Take this down to the dole office and tell them you've finished work.'

He don't look happy, and he won't look at me in the eyes. 'Do you know where the dole office is?'

He looks at me, but he don't give me a chance to answer. 'No, of course you don't.'

'Am I being a nuisance?'

Mr Jarvis grunts and bends over the plans with his back to us.

'No, of course not, Billy,' Mr Fred says, but I know it's not true. Sometimes I make a nuisance of myself, I know that. I try not to, but I'm a bit slow sometimes, and that annoys people.

Mr Fred picks up a blue phone book from the floor and flicks through the pages. There's loads and loads of names, and he runs his finger down the page looking for summat. His fingernail's all cracked and lined, like a wood shaving.

'Unemployment – see Employment. Typical!' He laughs and claps the book shut. 'The pink one, Billy. That's it – pass it over. Now, let's see.'

'We're closing now. You'll have to come back tomorrow.'

'Thank you, miss.'

She's got a nice face, but she looks tired. I stand up. I'm real stiff with all the sitting down.

'I live here.' I give her the card with my address on it. Mr Jackson wrote it for me. It's pretty handy sometimes, when I get lost like. 'How do I get home, please?'

She looks at the yellow card and then at me. 'Go out of

here and turn left. This way – ' She points. ' – and then along Westbourne Grove to the cinema, and then right again and you'll be there.'

I thank her and then go out. It's getting dark outside and the orange street lights have just come on. They're still flickery, like they're warming up. I'm pretty hungry now – I don't think I had any lunch. I can remember the way the girl told me to go, so I turn down the main street. I sort of recognise it, you know, some of the shops and that.

There's a chippy over the road, so I cross over careful and go in. It's good and warm inside and it smells great – all hot and salty. I love looking at the pies and stuff, all glittery in their plastic packs on the hot shelf.

I ask the girl for fish and chips and she makes a cone thing of paper and shoves them in. I stick loads of salt and vinegar on top – I like lots of that.

I go out and eat them on the street, but they're too hot at first, and I burn my mouth a bit. I huff on them to cool them down. I dunno if I want to eat them here, or walk and eat at the same time, but I think I know where I am, so I start walking. It's too blummin cold to hang round just eating chips.

It's a bit like Christmas. You know, like when it gets dark early, and everyone's wearing their winter clothes, and all the lights look pretty. And when you're eating good food as well.

One thing about eating chips I really like, you know, eating them from a bag on the street like, is how they warm up your hand. That's real good, that is.

Mr Vahidi's working on his stall, so I cross over and have a look. He's got a light bulb hanging over the stall – no shade or nothing, just a bulb – and it's pretty bright. It makes all the fruit and veg shine like those things they hang on Christmas trees, you know, those glass things.

An old bloke is buying some stuff – some tomatoes and funny long bean things. I think Mr Vahidi's real lucky to sell fruit and stuff – they look so good, like presents or summat. Except if they were presents, I wouldn't wrap them up – I'd give them just like they are.

The old bloke goes off and Mr Vahidi sees me.

'Fish and chips again, Billy?'

I look down at my hands. I'd forgot I was eating.

'Yes, Mr Vahidi.'

'It's not good for you all the time, this greasy food. You should eat some vegetables or your teeth will fall out.'

I give my front teeth a bit of a push to see if they're OK, but Mr Vahidi laughs. 'I was joking, Billy.' He turns round and picks up a big green apple and polishes it on his white coat. 'Here.'

It's cool and shiny, like it's been painted. It's real beautiful.

'Thank you, sir.'

I won't eat it. I'll put it on my dressing table and look at it. I stick it in my pocket and hold out the bag of chips.

'Chip, Mr Vahidi?'

The office is still smoky from yesterday. The windows are tight shut and the radiators are too hot to sit on, like they used to be at school. There's Shane from the building site, leaning forward in the orange plastic chair. He gobs on the floor and smears it with his boots. I sit in the same chair as yesterday. A man is shouting in the next room. I hate that, when people get angry and start shouting. It makes me scared. I wish people wouldn't do that.

'What's up, Billy?' Shane has turned round in his chair and is looking at me.

'Why are they arguing, Shane?'

'It's the only way to get anything out of the bastards, that's why.' He gets up and comes over to me. I'm a little bit afraid of Shane, to tell the truth.

'Don't have a fag on you?'

I shake my head.

'What number are you?' He sits down next to me.

I don't understand.

Shane nods at a counter thing over the desk. It's got

these big numbers on it that sometimes click over. I saw it yesterday.

Shane looks at a small bit of paper in his hand. 'Twenty-six. Only bloody twenty to go! Bastards – look at them behind their glass case! They'll make you wait all day just to make sure you deserve it.'

I can smell Shane's clothes. He smells sort of dusty. You get real dusty carrying bricks around. He ain't shaved for a couple of days, and to tell the truth he looks a bit scruffy. He's got a tattoo of a bluebird on his wrist. I can't see it now, cos his sleeves are down, but I know he's got it cos he showed it to me. It's pretty nice, I reckon. I wouldn't mind having a tattoo of a bluebird.

He calls over to a young woman wearing this red head-scarf. There's a pushchair next to her, but it's empty. 'Got a fag, luv?'

She shakes her head. She don't look too happy.

'Bitch!' Shane says to me. 'I bet she has.'

Shane's losing his temper. He bangs on the thick glass in front of him.

'So, tell me – what am I supposed to do? Sleep in the park?'

I can't hear the answer, I can only see the young man behind the glass move his lips.

'Why don't you just admit it – you don't give a shit!'

Shane jumps up. He catches the back of his legs on the chair and swears, and then hurries out. The woman with the head-scarf watches him go. She looks a bit scared. I look at the bloke behind the glass. His face is white and tired, and he takes off his glasses to rub his eyes. The counter clicks and an old man gets up.

I think for a bit, then I get up and go out. Shane's in the street. He's real angry still.

'What am I supposed to do now?' he asks me. 'They won't give me an emergency payment cos I've just been paid – it makes no difference to those fuckers that I'm broke. How am I supposed to pay for a room with – ' He

7

digs in his pockets and pulls out some coins. 'Thirty-five pence?'

There's an old man sitting on the doorstep by us. I saw him yesterday. I think he's drunk or summat cos he's talking to himself. Sort of swearing.

'Stay with me,' I say to Shane.

'What do you mean?'

'Stay with me. I got a room.'

He looks at me for a bit, like he's thinking about it, then he grins. He takes hold of my arm and turns me round. 'Lead on, son.'

I like the reflections of the bottles in the mirror. Some bottles let the light through and sort of spears of colour – green, orange, red – light up the middle of the reflection.

I like the green one best. Once on the beach I found a round bit of glass – the bottom of a bottle I think it was. Its edges were all smooth and the glass was speckled and sort of misty. When I looked through it everything swirled in green like it does when you look through a spangle or summat.

'Can I have that bottle, please?'

'You want a whole bottle of gin?' The man sounds surprised.

'Don't take any notice of him.' Shane taps his head and rolls his eyes. 'He's a bit thick.' Shane's lips are wet from the beer and his eyes are shiny.

I go red and look at my glass. I don't like it when people say things like that. I sort of get embarrassed. People think I'm thick and always say things like that. But it's not true – I'm just a bit slow.

There's nothing wrong with asking the man for the bottle. I thought it might be empty and he was going to chuck it away or summat. If you don't ask, you don't get – that's what Mr Browne used to say. I don't think it's fair for Shane to say I'm thick just cos I asked for the bottle.

8

I can't drink any more beer. I don't really like it. I've never been in a pub before and I didn't know what to ask for, so I had the same as Shane. I wish I had lemonade or summat instead – I don't really like this beer. Shane's drinking whisky with his beer, and I pick up the glass and swirl it round a bit. It looks nice, but it tastes real horrible. I dunno how anybody can drink that stuff.

Shane can just fit on the floor between the end of the bed and the dresser. I got a spare blanket Mrs Riley gave me, so he's using that. He didn't get undressed or nothing – he just took off his boots and jacket. He's using his jacket as a pillow, which is a pretty good idea I think, cos I only got one. He's talking loud like I'm a long way away, and he's using my avocado plant for an ashtray.

'What do you want all these bloody plants for?' He pulls it towards him and starts twitching one of the leaves. It's a nice plant – I grew it from a seed and it's got quite a few leaves on it now. He gives a yank and pulls the biggest leaf off.

'I mean – ' He belches real loud. 'Jesus Christ, I'm pissed!'

I get out of bed. I ain't got nothing on, except my pants like, and it's flipping cold. I pick up the plant and shove it on the dressing table out of Shane's reach. The apple Mr Vahidi gave me is still there. I sort of brush it with my fingers, and imagine biting into it. I shiver and hop back into bed.

'You're a weird bugger – you know that?'

From my bed I can just see Shane's toes – not his top half at all. His big toe's pushed through a hole in his sock, and I look at it for a bit.

'Hey! Keep the fucking light on!'

I smile and tuck my legs up. It's like school, having someone to sleep with.

I wake up just as the door comes open. Someone switches the light on and I have to shut my eyes, it's so bright.

'What's going on here?' It's Mrs Riley. 'Why aren't you at work? And who's this?'

I sit up in bed and try and get my eyes open. I don't know what she's going on about. Then I remember.

'It's Shane, Mrs Riley.'

'So that's what all the racket was last night! I told you when you moved in I wouldn't have people staying overnight. This is a single bedsitting room. I'll have to charge you double if two of you stay.'

Mrs Riley tugs open the curtains. It's grey outside, and it's been raining. I can see streaks of rain down the window.

'And why aren't you at work?' She switches the light off and turns to look at me.

'There's no more work, Mrs Riley.'

It's cold and I pull the sheets up to my neck. Shane still ain't moved.

She's angry – I can see by her eyes. 'And how are you going to pay the rent then? I told that social worker fellow I won't have DHSS claimants staying here. Come on you.' She sort of kicks Shane's foot. 'Get up.'

'And what's this mess?'

Shane must've knocked the avocado off the dresser cos there's soil all over the lino. 'Come on you – get up.'

Shane groans and pulls the blanket over his head.

'Was it you I heard being sick in the toilet last night?'

He don't say nothing, so she looks at me again. 'Look, young man. I can't have you staying here if you can't pay. I can get good money for this room.'

Mrs Riley is wearing her flowery apron – pink and blue flowers the same colour as them bushes by the sea. She's got another one – a red one with white dots on it, but I don't like it so much as this one. I like this one cos it reminds me of them bushes. I spect that's why Mrs Riley bought it – cos she likes flowers and that.

'Do you understand me, young man?'

To tell the truth I wasn't really following what she was saying, so I just sort of look like I was listening.

10

'I've got some money in the Post Office,' I say.

She looks surprised. 'You've got some savings then?'

'Yes, Mrs Riley.' Mr Jackson helped me save up the money they gave me at the building site. I go to the Post Office every Saturday and stick some in my Post Office book. It's a blue one with my name on it. I think about getting out of bed and showing her the book, but I ain't got no pyjamas on, and she might tell me off.

'Shall I go to the Post Office and get you some money?'

She thinks for a bit. 'You do that, Billy. But it's no good if you've no job to go to – your savings won't last for ever you know.'

'I know, Mrs Riley.'

'Now, both of you. Up and out – I want to clean up this mess.'

'How much money have I got, Shane?'

He takes the Post Office book from me and flicks through the pages.

'£403. You're rich, Billy.'

'Is that a lot?'

'Enough to get you pissed every night for a month.'

'Can you show me how to fill in the form please? I can't quite remember.'

He looks at the paper I give him. 'Name here, account number here, how much you want here.'

I can write my name and that, so I copy it from the book onto the form. It takes me a bit of time, but I manage it in the end and show Shane what I've wrote.

'Is that right?'

'Christ, Billy! Is that the best you can do? Your B is backwards.'

I look at the form, trying to find the B.

'Can't you write at all? I thought *I* was thick. Here – let me do it.'

Shane screws up the first bit of paper and takes another. I watch him over his shoulder. It's like magic, how the ink comes out so quick onto the paper.

'How much do you want? All of it?'

'OK.'

'Sign your name here.' He shoves the paper across to me.

I write my name again, careful with the B this time.

'You wait here and I'll get the money.'

It's a pretty long queue so I lean against the counter and watch the people waiting. I can still taste the breakfast on my teeth – sausages and egg and fried bread. We had a good breakfast, me and Shane.

I watch him for a bit. He looks pretty miserable standing there with his jacket all damp across the shoulders. I have a think about his bluebird tattoo. It's pretty good – I saw it again last night when we was in the pub. I wouldn't mind having a tattoo like that. But it might hurt a bit though. They use needles to make the tattoo. That must hurt a bit, I reckon.

'Here we go, Billy. Four hundred quid.'

Shane hands me some notes.

'Now you go back and give that old bag what's for. I'm going to be off.'

I fold the money into the Post Office book careful like, and tuck the book into my back pocket.

'What's this?'

'Four hundred pounds, Mrs Riley.'

'Billy – it's twenty.'

We sort of stare at each other. I dunno what to say. Mrs Riley's just finished eating lunch, and there's a piece of food stuck in her false teeth.

'You didn't give any to that friend of yours?'

'He didn't want any.'

'Let me see that book.'

She takes the blue book from me and looks through it.

'Oh Billy – you stupid – ' she whispers. 'Did you get the money, or did he?'

'Shane did.'

'You've been robbed – you know that?'

12

She's angry now. 'Look, Billy – this is twenty pounds. Five, ten, fifteen, twenty.' She counts them out one by one. 'This won't keep you going for a week!'

I sort of shrug and stick my hands in my pockets. Mrs Riley sighs and looks at me.

'Look, I can't have you staying here any more. I've been good to you, but I'm not qualified to look after somebody like you. You should be in some sort of home.'

I watch her hair when she's talking. The top bit is a wig. It's the same colour as a Ginger Nut biscuit. I want to give it a feel, but I try and concentrate on what she's saying.

'I've got no choice. I'll have to give you a week's notice.'

I don't understand what she means, and she shuts her eyes for a sec. Then she opens them and looks straight at me.

'I want you out by next Friday.'

I kneel on the edge of my brown suitcase and click the lock shut. The new man is sitting on the bed watching me.

'Is that everything, then? Did you check the cupboard?' Mrs Riley's got a big bunch of keys on a steel ring in her hand.

'You can't take all your plants, Billy. Be sensible – choose just one of them. You'll never be able to carry them all.'

I choose my favourite – the one with the red and green leaves – and stick it on top of my clothes in the carrier bag. I want to take the rest, but I can't, so I just look at them for a bit. I really like my plants. It's a shame to leave them behind.

'Where are you off to now, Billy?' Mr McDonald's in the hall, making a phone call. I look at his feet. He's wearing brown leather shoes without laces.

'Feet better, Mr McDonald?'

'Not so bad.' He nods at the case. 'Are you moving out?'

'Yes, sir.'

'Where to?'

'I dunno.'

Mr McDonald puts the phone down and looks at Mrs Riley. The hall light's shining off the silver pen in his top pocket, sort of winking at me.

'Why's he going?'

'That's a matter between me and Billy.'

'You mean you're booting him out in the middle of the night, with nowhere to go?'

He's like the doctor at school – how he used to talk to Mr Browne. You know, sort of ignoring me.

'He's had a week to find somewhere.'

Mr McDonald clicks his tongue. He don't like Mrs Riley.

'So, what are you going to do, Billy?'

I'm feeling uncomfortable. My shoelaces are tied too tight, and my feet itch.

'Have you got any money?'

'Yes, sir.' I pull a blue note out of my back pocket and show him.

'Is that all?'

I give the coins in my pocket a rattle. Mr McDonald looks serious for a moment and I think he's going to tell me off.

'I'll write down the address of a hostel. You go straight there, and tomorrow you tell them you're broke. OK?'

Mrs Riley's gone back into the room, and I can hear her talking to the new man. Mr McDonald looks through the phone book and writes summat on the back of a taxi card.

'It's in Paddington. Now you go to the tube – you know where that is, don't you?'

'Yes, sir.'

'It's just one stop to Paddington. When you get there, get out and show someone this address.'

He gives me the little card. It's stiff and new. The writing makes a pattern like a thread of cotton all bunched up.

'Good luck, son.'

Mrs Riley's back in the hall and Mr McDonald looks at her. 'I hope you find somewhere half-way decent,' he says, and sort of tilts his head like a bird. 'Now, you'd better be off before it closes.'

The stairs are like silverfish – like the one I found in the bath once. I grab a hold of the black handrail. It judders under my hand like it's alive. It's a weird feeling going down this staircase without walking or nothing. I been on these stairs before, but it's still pretty weird. It's like sinking, this going down past all the lights and posters. I don't mind it – it's pretty good fun, but it makes me feel a bit dizzy. I have a bit of trouble at the bottom – you know, where the steps go into the ground. I get off OK but my case falls over and the stairs push it like it's a bit of driftwood. Someone steps round it, and they nearly bump into me.

I get my case sorted out and stand there a bit, watching the people coming down the stairs. Some of them don't move. They're like those dummies in the shops – you know, not moving, but looking real like. These two blokes bounce down the stairs like a couple of horses. They must be in a real hurry, cos they run past me and on down the corridor.

There's a fag end on the last step, twitching and jumping like it's alive. I pick it up and move it onto the concrete. There.

I find the train place in the end and wait for the train to come. It's pretty interesting here. I've been on a train before, but not on my own like. I sit on my suitcase and look at the adverts stuck on the wall. There's one of a little kid dancing on a table – a girl, like. She looks real excited about summat. I dunno what she's all excited about, but it looks like it's her birthday or summat.

When the train comes, it's so fast and noisy it scares me a bit and I put my hands over my ears till it stops. It sighs when it stops and then the doors jerk open. It's warm inside and the seats are nice with their red leather edges. I dunno if I should sit down, cos it's only one stop, but I do in the end. There ain't many people in the train, so there's loads of seats to spare.

When the train starts off, it goes slow and then quicker and all the posters on the platform go past real quick, then we go into the tunnel. I watch the straps sway for a bit. It's like invisible people are hanging there, swinging them. I can see myself in the glass opposite – two of me. It's like looking into water.

It's like the cave I been in once with the school. All the sounds are all sort of echoey like. I can hear some music when I follow the people along the platform, and when we come out into this big hall place I can see it's two girls playing violins. It's real beautiful, the music they're making, sort of soft and complicated like. There's two of them playing, and the music sort of winds together, first one then the other, like – I dunno – like climbing stairs one foot at a time.

The girls are wearing duffle coats and they look real warm and happy. One of them's got long hair and it sort of hangs down and dances with the music. They don't really notice no one. They're too busy watching the sheet of paper on the stand in front of them, and playing their violins. Sometimes people chuck money in a bag they've got, and the girls smile real polite like, but they don't stop playing. I'd really like to play the violin – it sounds so blummin beautiful.

Sometimes I see things – you know, just little things – or hear music and stuff like that, and it's like I can't believe it. I know it's for real, but it's like really special and . . . *new*. You know, like I've never seen it before, or never heard nothing ever before. Sort of like a dream or summat. I dunno – it's hard to explain.

When the girls stop to chat, or change the piece of paper, it's funny, but I can still hear the music.

I try to clap when they stop, but I'm carrying my bag and I can't clap proper. It's funny that, but no one stops to listen. Sometimes they chuck money in the bag, but they

16

don't stop. I suppose people are real busy, or in a hurry to get home. I can't understand that – they don't even stop for *one* minute.

'You're dropping things.'

The girl with the long hair's talking to me, and I look down at my feet. The carrier bag's split and some stuff's fallen out – my hairbrush and a pair of socks. The girls have stopped playing now. I think they're going home, cos they're packing up and putting their violins in their cases.

I try and stuff my things back in my bag and watch the girls at the same time, but the split gets bigger and more stuff falls out and by the time I get it all back in they've gone.

I dunno what to do now. I've forgot what I've got to do. There's no one around and so I sit on my case for a bit. I can still hear the music, specially if I shut my eyes. I wish they were still here – I thought that music was blummin beautiful.

'Last train's gone. Come on – we're locking up.'

I open my eyes with a start. There's a black man with a hat like a bus conductor in front of me. I stand up and pick up my carrier bag, but stuff falls out the bottom. The man don't help me stick it back in – he just watches me. Then I remember the card Mr McDonald gave me. I feel in my pocket for it and show the man.

'Can you tell me how to get here please, sir?'

He takes the card and turns it round so he can read it.

'This is in Paddington, son. It's quite a walk.' He's got a couple of gold teeth, and they shine in his mouth like jewelry.

'Where am I, please?'

'Notting Hill Gate.'

The man's looking at me with a question on his face. 'You can get a night bus to Paddington, but – ' he shakes his head, 'if it's a hostel, it'll be shut now anyway.'

The man gave me a new placky bag – a big white one with a picture of a turkey on it. It's flipping cold outside, and

17

dark as well. The man padlocks the gate behind me, and we say goodnight to each other. I spect he's going home to his wife now.

It's been raining and the lights on the pavement are all fuzzy. I watch the lights for a bit. There's a green one going on and off, like a fairground light. I hold my breath when it's off and breathe when it's on. There ain't too many people about. There's a few cars on the street going by, but it ain't like there's people in them. I can't see them – the people, that is – and they ain't going to stop anyhow. The cars are like sort of animals, hissing by on the road – big white eyes coming close and red ones going away. A lorry turns down the road past me. I can see the driver. He's smoking a fag. I can see the teeny red star as he drives past.

The pavements are wide and empty like a beach. It's pretty windy and I stop and watch a ball of litter roll round and round like a dog chasing its tail. Round and round it goes.

It's real cold now. I got my gloves on, but my hands are real cold. I huff on them to warm them up, and for a minute they feel all wet, like there's water running through my fingers.

There's a man and a woman crossing the road by the lights, so I follow them. They're walking pretty slow – she's got her hand in his coat pocket. I catch up with them and walk behind them for a bit. Her coat's got a fur collar, and it shivers in the wind like a real animal. I spect they've been to a party or summat – they look real smart, like they're wearing party clothes.

The suitcase is pretty heavy and I stop now and then to have a rest. It ain't so bright here, away from all the shops. The street lights are on, but they're all yellowy and not as bright as the shop lights. I look round at the houses. Most of them are dark and asleep, but there's lights on in one or two windows. I suppose it must be pretty late.

Suddenly I get my urge to shout, but I stop myself.

Sometimes it happens, you know. I just get this urge to shout summat, but I don't do it cos it ain't polite to make a lot of noise. Specially in the middle of the night cos people might be sleeping. So what I do is grab my suitcase and start running down the pavement – real fast, as fast as I can.

The trees are like black giants. Sort of leaning against the sky with their arms out, stretching up to the moon. I think for a bit there's a waterfall, but then I realise it's the wind through the trees. It sounds like water. The moon's come out from the clouds and it's pretty bright now. I can see some stars.

There's a lot of grass, like a field or summat with this old tree in the middle. It's like an old spiky witch – it ain't got no leaves, just these spiky twig things, and it looks like a million fingers all pointing in different directions. I rub my hand over its trunk. The bark's rough and cold, like a real old conker. There's a hole in the middle – burnt out probably by kids with firelighters. I spect there's an animal living in there. They often do that you know – live inside old trees and that.

Suddenly there's this loud screech, and I nearly jump out of my skin. It's a bird or summat, but at first I thought it was a person. It sounded like that – you know, like a person screaming.

I go over and have a look at the building I can see. It looks pretty old, a bit like one of them mansion things. You know – big and sort of like a castle. I don't think no one lives here, cos there's no lights on. I try some of the windows, but they're all locked, so I squash my nose up against the glass and pull faces at a pretend person on the other side. After I do that for a bit, I decide to have a look round. It's some sort of garden I reckon – there's loads of flowerbeds, but they're all empty. They probably digged them out for the winter. That's what they do – dig out the old stuff, store the bulbs and that, and then shove new stuff in. Winter stuff. I stick my fingers in the soil. It feels like good stuff, rich like with all them leaves rotting and mulching down. Nice and peaty. It's a good garden, this – well, good if they stuck the winter stuff in, and stuff like that.

I try a door to this building and it comes open, so I go in. It's like a greenhouse – you know, all glass and that. It sort of smells of plants too – a bit like that big greenhouse place we went with the school. The one with all them palm trees and stuff.

It's quiet in here – there's no wind or nothing. It's nice and warm too. The moonlight's shining through the windows, sort of flickery through the leaves. It looks like the sea, the light on the floor – you know, the moving bits of light on the top of waves you see.

I dump the bags down by the door and have a look round. It's hard to see much. It's still pretty dark, even with the moonlight. I take a couple of steps, then I get a hell of a shock. I can see people all over the place. For a second I get all confused and that, and then I see they ain't people. They're statues. It must be one of them gallery things. There's a big head on a stand, with the moon shining smack in its face. Once I got over my shock I ain't afraid, and have a wander round. I give the head thing a feel. It's funny like – I expected summat soft – you know, like a real head, but this is hard and all rough like. I can stick my fingers in the middle of its eyes. There's little holes there just the size of my finger. Then I nearly bump into a little girl made of some shiny metal stuff. She's about the age of Annie – the same size like – just up to my knee. She's got this cute little pony tail and a fat little face. Real cute, like. It looks like she's smiling at me, but it's hard to tell in the dark. Over the other side, there's some sort of dancer, and she's got no blummin clothes on. She's not very big. She's grown up and that, but she's no bigger than a kid. She just about comes up to my chest. Her arms are over her head, showing off her armpits and her boobies. I want to touch her, she's so pretty, but I'm not allowed to touch. And anyway, she's

20

all naked. She's got a real lovely body, though. I'd like to see her dance.

Then I see this white one. There's spots of moonlight over her and she's all white and smooth like she's all soapy and stuff. She's lying on a rock, but it ain't a real rock, cos I feel it and it's hollow. It feels sort of plasticky. But blimey, her body looks really real. It's real clever how they make summat look so real. This one's small and that, and she ain't got no clothes on neither. I squat down and have a look. I really want to touch her, so that's what I do. I just sort of hold my fingers against her side for a sec. It's weird, cos she's all cold. I expected her to feel warm, cos she looks so real, like. But she's real smooth – bloody beautiful. Her hair's all over one arm and her eyes are shut like she's asleep. I run my fingers over her face and her eyes and mouth and that. Her neck is real nice – like a real girl's neck – you know, all soft and nice looking. I put my hand over her shoulder and stroke it a bit, like she's a dog or summat, then I run my hand down her side and her legs, right down to her feet. I pretend I'm tickling her feet, like she's a real person and I'm a mate of hers. She's bloody beautiful, I reckon. Her tummy and boobies are real smooth. I want to put my face close to her, but I'm embarrassed like, so I stare at her for a long time and don't do nothing. Then I sort of rest my face against her tummy. One of her boobies is all lit up with the moon, and it looks like a real person. She's so real I can smell her skin – it smells all soapy and clean like. I wish she was my girlfriend. I want to pick her up and give her a cuddle, but she won't move – she's stuck to the rock or summat. Anyway, she won't budge, so I go and get my bags and dump them down near her. Suddenly I get a good idea, and take the plant out of the placky bag.

'Miss,' I say, all polite like. 'I would be honoured if you would accept this plant from me, Mr Billy Bayswater.'

It's silly like, but I imagine her talking back to me. 'Well, thank you, sir. It's just what I wanted. Please put it by my boudoir.'

I give a little bow and stick it on the floor by her head. It's pretty warm, so I just lie down next to her, and stick the placky bag under my head for a pillow. I watch her for a few minutes, and then I start getting tired so I say goodnight to her and shut my eyes.

It's like being in a jungle or summat, that light flickering through the leaves. Or being under water. I'm pretty stiff from lying on the floor, but I don't move or nothing. I just lie there a bit, watching the lights flashing over the ceiling. When I first woke up, I was a bit confused where I was, but when I saw the girl I remembered. The room looks different from last night, but the girl's still real pretty – even whiter than last night. I'm still pretty sleepy, so I lie back and just look at the roof, and the lights waving through the leaves. The sunlight's all flickery, but I keep my eyes open all the same. I can see little red flashes like fireworks going off, and I shut my eyes, but I can still see them. Then I go all tight, and I know I'm going to have a fit. I try and control myself, but it's too late and it's like I'm falling backwards, and the lights keep flashing.

'What the bloody hell do you think you're doing?'

I can see him well enough, but I can't get no sound out, so I just have to stare up at him. He looks a long way off.

'How did you get in here?'

I can feel the sweat on my forehead and my head aches like mad. I try and say summat, but I can't get my mouth to work.

'What's wrong with you?'

I wish he'd go away and leave me a bit, but he squats down and sticks his face right up to mine. I push myself up on one elbow. My head hurts like anything, and the room sort of spins round for a while. I try to say summat to the man, but only weird sounds come out.

'Come on you, up you get.'

He pulls me to my feet and I look down at the girl, but

22

she ain't moved. I feel a bit embarrassed at having a fit in front of the girl. She might think I'm stupid or summat, having a fit like that just for nothing. The man takes me outside and sits me down on this wooden bench.

'You stay here,' he says. I shut my eyes and try and stop my head from thumping. I hate these fits. They make me feel so ill after.

The other man wouldn't believe me when I said I just opened the door last night and walked in. He went round all the windows checking to make sure I hadn't broke in. In the end he comes back to the bench and tells me off, saying this is private property and that. I didn't do no harm, but still he told me off.

I feel a bit better now. I still got a bit of a headache, but not so bad as before. I'm starving, so I go in the little caff round the corner from the glasshouse. There's tables outside in this little yard thing, but it's too flipping cold to sit outside, so I go in and sit by the window. It's not a proper caff – they don't do breakfast like, but they have bread and tea and stuff. I buy a pork pie and a cup of tea and I feel better after I've ate summat.

This place is a park or summat – there's loads of trees and flowerbeds and stuff, but they're all empty except for a few rose bushes. I get another cup of tea and just sort of sit and stare out the window. I like it here – just watching people working on the flowerbeds, raking the soil and picking up leaves and that.

The girl in the caff runs after me and tells me I've forgot my bags, so I go back and fetch them. The suitcase is getting heavy, but I go back and fetch it all the same. It's got my name on it, which is pretty useful I suppose.

There's an old bloke working on the flowerbed. He's wearing these green wellies and he's just sort of walking up and down the bed, squashing the soil down. I ask if I can help him and he looks at me funny. He's got a blue boilersuit and a scarf round his neck.

'If you want a job you'll need to see the head gardener,

Mr Fielding. You'll find him in the office over there.' He points to a building.

I think about that for a minute, but I can't figure it out so I ask him what he's doing.

'Treading the earth ready for planting.'

It looks pretty easy so I sort of try with one foot on the grass and one foot on the flowerbed. I just sort of squash the soil down, like the man's doing.

'Can I give you a hand, sir?'

He stops his treading and looks at me. It looks like he's going to say no, but he nods instead.

'OK. Start in that corner and we'll meet in the middle.'

It feels great, walking on this soil – it sort of gives under my feet, like walking on dry sand. I do it as careful as I can so he'll be pleased.

When we're finished he picks up his rake and starts raking another bed, but I can't see why – there ain't any leaves or stuff to rake up. It looks like fun. The rake makes a pattern on the surface like when you comb your hair when it's still wet. Sort of wavy lines. When he's finished he comes over to me.

'Look son, haven't you got anything better to do?' He looks a bit worried.

'Can I help, please?' I ask again.

He breathes in sharp, like he's smoking a cigarette. Then he sort of frowns at me.

He nods at my suitcase. 'Are you off someplace?'

I don't understand.

'Moving?'

'No, sir,' I say. He's got a little dribble of snot on the end of his nose, like some old folks do. I want to give him my hanky to wipe it, but I know it ain't polite, so I don't.

'Where are you living?'

That one stops me and I think hard, but I can't get an answer, so I just sort of shrug.

'Are you the one that stayed in the Orangery last night?'

I don't know what an Orangery is, so I look at my feet.

'That place over there.'

I look to where he's pointing and see the glasshouse. I remember now.

'Yes sir. That's where I'm living.'

'You can't – ' he starts to say, then he stops. He looks at his watch all of a sudden and then drops the rake down. 'It's my tea break now. You come along with me.'

I follow him to a side building and into a small room. It's cosy here – there's an electric kettle and a little stove and everything. A couple of blokes in boots and blue boilersuits are sitting on a table, drinking out of mugs.

'Where's Jack? This lad here needs a job.'

One of the men looks at me. 'We've got a full quota, mate. They're not taking on anyone else.'

I need to go, so I ask for the toilet. The old bloke shows me. When I get back everyone looks at me funny. There's a new man there, the oldest of the lot.

'Have a cup of tea,' he says, nodding at the kettle and tea bags and stuff. I can feel him watching me while I make it.

'I'm afraid there's no work.'

I'm concentrating on pouring out the hot water, so I only half listen to him.

'Eddie here says you've got no place to stay.'

I don't say nothing – just poke the tea bag round in the water, hoping they're going to stop asking me questions.

'What's your name, son?'

I smile at that one and look up at him – that's easy. 'Billy, sir.'

'I don't mind if you help out, but you have to understand we can't pay you.'

I warm my hands on the mug. 'Thank you, sir.'

The old man looks at me a bit doubtful like, but then he smiles out the corner of his mouth. I like him.

I help Mr Fielding the rest of the morning. He's a nice bloke. He don't talk too much or nothing like that. He just gives me a rake and that and tells me what to do.

There's loads of leaves to rake up – piles of them, all dry and brown like bits of scorched paper. I rake them into a great heap and then a yellow tractor with a trailer thing comes round and I help shove all the leaves in the back. There's loads of them. I ask where they're going – I hoped we'd have a bonfire and that – but the man says they'll be taken away someplace and got rid of.

It's pretty cold, but I got my gloves on and my woolly hat, and it ain't too bad. I want to rake the soil like the man did in the morning, so Mr Fielding shows me a flowerbed and tells me what to do. The soil's pretty black and there's no stones or stuff like the gardens at school.

I do the job the best I can, making the same wavy lines like the other bloke did. It's a lot of fun doing this. It's nice stuff, this black soil.

I got a bit of money left, so I have lunch with a couple of them in the caff. I have soup and bread and a slice of pie. They're all friendly like, joking and smoking fags and stuff – like Mr Fred and the others on the building site.

In the afternoon a load of plants turn up and they start planting them in the beds. I want to help, but it looks a bit complicated, so I get on and rake more leaves.

It's pretty dark in the afternoon – not like night's coming, but just sort of grey like it's going to rain anytime. It don't rain – it just feels like it will. I don't mind this – raking up leaves. It ain't too difficult, and I like the look of them. Some of them are still greeny, but most are brown. I sometimes find some really nice red ones and I stick them in my pocket. It seems a shame to chuck away summat that's so beautiful.

They've got squirrels here – little darty grey things that run across the grass in spurts, and then stop and twitch ever so slightly. Some of them are real tame. They come up to you and twitch their noses and flick their tails and sit up like they're begging for food. I wish I got some food to give them, cos I spect they're hungry. One of them comes up real close to me. He's really pretty – his tail's all fluffed up and delicate like a feather, and he just sits there, all nervous and twitchy waiting for me to give him summat to eat. Mr Fielding says they save up food for the winter. That seems a good idea – saving up food so they don't have to go out in the snow. Some animals are real clever.

I spend most of the afternoon on my own, but I don't mind. Sometimes Mr Fielding comes over to see I'm OK, but most of the time I'm all alone. I carry on working till it gets dark, and Mr Fielding comes over to me. It's the sort of day when you want to go inside and have tea with the lights on, and then sit in the warm looking out the window.

'So, where are you going to stay, Billy?'

It's funny, but for a minute, seeing him standing there with the lights on in the building behind him I think I'm back at school and it's Mr Browne not Mr Fielding I'm talking to. I look at him, and then behind him at the building. It looks cosy in there, with all the lights on.

'Well, Billy?'

I dunno what to say. It's complicated sometimes, when people ask you questions and you don't know what to say. I look like I'm thinking so he won't ask me again, but to tell the truth I can't remember what he said.

'Look. If you promise to behave yourself, you can stay in the office for tonight.'

It's really dark now. I can hardly see Mr Fielding's face.

'And then tomorrow you go off and get yourself a proper place – the social services should be able to find you somewhere. You can't go on sleeping in the office for ever.'

'Thank you, sir,' I say. He takes the rake from me and we walk back together. Then he stops and slaps his forehead like they do in films when they've forgot summat or they've done summat silly.

'It's Sunday tomorrow – I won't be into work.'

He sighs and looks at me. The light from the building shines off his eyeballs making them look all slimy. 'And the social services'll be shut.'

He sort of taps me on the arm. 'Never mind. You'll have to stay till Monday. I'll pop over tomorrow to see you're all right.'

The office is nice with all the tools and stuff. It's quiet though. Places always seem quieter just after people go – like they've taken all the sound away. But they left the light on and showed me where the switch is. Mr Fielding told me not to use the stove just in case I have an accident. He said I could have the electric fire on, but I dunno how to work it.

I'm blummin starving, but there ain't no food – just tea bags and a bit of milk. I drink the milk and chuck the carton away. It's all right here – it's pretty interesting. There's a sink, and I run some cold water for summat to do. Then I switch it off and sit on the table and just sort of swing my legs like the blokes did. There's a mirror over the sink and I hop down and have a look at myself in it. It's funny looking in a mirror. You never see yourself unless you look in a mirror. You walk around all day with the same face, but you're the only one who don't see it. If you didn't have a mirror, you'd never know what you looked like. That's pretty odd, I reckon.

I pull some faces at myself in the mirror, just to see what I look like when I pull faces. It's pretty funny.

I don't really feel tired, even though it's been dark for ages. I pick up one of the spades and pretend I'm digging the floor. I ain't really, cos it's wood, but I just pretend. It's a nice spade – it's pretty new. It's got a green plastic handle and the spade bit is all metal – all shiny and new looking.

After I do that for a while I get bored and put the spade back with the rest of the stuff. I crumble some soil from one of the rakes in my fingers. It's all dry now. It feels nice, and pretty clean in a funny way. Then I just sort of mess around for a bit, looking at things and stuff. It's real quiet and I hold my breath so I can listen proper, but I can't hear nothing.

Sometimes I get lonely when there's no one around. I get out my plant from my placky bag and give it a look. It looks pretty dry, so I give it some water from the tap and then I put it on the side. I really like this plant. It's got these red and green leaves, and it feels sort of warm and furry. After I look at it for a bit I start talking to it. I know it's pretty silly, but that's what I do. Sometimes I do that, you know – talk to my plants like you talk to a dog or summat. Sometimes I think plants can hear you like dogs and cats can. I know it's pretty silly, but sometimes I do that – you know, talk to them for a bit. I only do it when I'm on my own, though.

Anyway, after that I sort of make a bed for myself. I take off my coat and lie down on it and use the placky bag for a pillow. I leave the light on, not cos I don't know where the switch is – I do, Mr Fielding showed me, but cos sometimes when I'm in a new place I like to see where I am just in case I wake up and want a look. It's still pretty cold, so after a bit I get up and change my coat so it's on top of me like a blanket. The floor's pretty dusty and that, but I ain't got nothing else to lie on, so I just have to hope I don't get too dirty.

It's not so comfy as last night, and I feel a bit lonely, to tell the truth. I even cry for a bit, but then I get tired and I go to sleep.

Mr Fielding's the kindest person I ever met – except for Mr Browne. He came early this morning and took me to the caff for breakfast. I was blummin starving and pretty cold too, so I had two bowls of soup and a pork pie. We just sat there, me and Mr Fielding, chatting like. He told me that Mrs Fielding wasn't too well. She's got summat wrong with her chest, and she coughs a lot and stuff. But he's real kind, Mr Fielding is, cos after brekky he took me back to the office and we got out some tools and a tray of plants and he took me to a flowerbed and showed me what to do. First we made a hole in the ground with a trowel, then we stuck the plants in and sort of scooped the earth back so they're cosy like. He watched me for a bit to make sure I was doing it right, then he said he'll be back later and went off.

I jumped when he opened the door first thing this morning. It was so quiet, and then suddenly the door opens. It was a bit of a shock at first, but when I seen it was Mr Fielding I was real glad. I like Mr Fielding. He's a nice bloke, I reckon. It was pretty early when he came. It wasn't night no more, but it wasn't day proper neither. Just sort of in the middle. I'd been awake for a while, cos I hadn't really slept all that well on the floor. It wasn't too comfy to tell the truth, and it was flipping cold as well. So I was real glad to see Mr Fielding.

It was a while before the caff opened, so he said he'd show me round. It's a blummin big park, and there's loads of animals and birds and stuff. There was these peacocks too. The man ones had these real long tails, sort of dragging behind them, and we saw one of them hold his tail up like a huge fan and sort of rattle it. That was real good, that was. Mr Fielding showed me the woman peacocks, and I was real surprised cos they didn't really look like peacocks at all – they're more like big chickens or summat – you know, all brown and normal looking. They was real interesting though. We saw loads of other things too – squirrels and rabbits and that. There was a big bird Mr Fielding wanted to show me. I can't remember its name, but we couldn't see it. It was probably still asleep or summat. I never knew there was all these animals and birds here. I just thought it was a flower park with grass and stuff. Anyway, I really like it. It's real interesting.

It was real misty, like it gets on some mornings, and when we come out of the animal place, there was all this mist just sort of hanging over the grass, and some trees in the middle sticking up like they was islands in a sea or summat. It was real beautiful and when you breathed in, you could feel the wet in your nose, like when you have a steamy bath. Mr Fielding just sort of walked on and when he turns round and sees I ain't moving he asks me what

I'm looking at. I couldn't explain, so I just sort of pointed. Anyway, Mr Fielding didn't understand, so back he comes and turns round so he can look proper. Then he says, 'Yes, it's nice, Billy,' sort of like it's normal or summat. 'Come on,' he says, but I won't budge. So then I says, 'Look, Mr Fielding'. And then it's like summat happens to him. His face changes and he gives a sort of sigh and I know he's looking proper, like. We just stand there a long time, our breath coming out like steam. We don't say nothing – we just look. It was so peaceful – no traffic or nothing, just bird sounds and the mist hanging over the grass.

I'm busy putting the flowers in and stuff. I been at it ages now, but I don't mind. I'm enjoying this. I've used up one box of plants already. They're not really flowers – they're mostly just green, but some of them have got these pretty blue flowers on. I'm doing a pretty good job I reckon. Mr Fielding's going to be pleased with me I reckon. He's going to think I'm real grown up for doing it so neat and careful.

There's a couple of people and dogs around now. One little dog rushes over to me and sniffs me all interested like, and has a look to see what I'm doing. He sniffs around a bit more and then he darts off, like he's satisfied I'm doing a good job.

I like this. I ain't too cold or nothing, and I like the feel of the soil in my fingers. Some people don't understand plants. They just think they're pretty. You know, just good for looking at. But they're like having a pet or summat – you know, you got to feed them and look after them and stuff. They start off small, and then they grow and then they get old and die. But some people just think they're . . . *things*, you know – not alive at all.

This girl comes over and watches me a bit. I don't say nothing to her, I just carry on with my job. After the mist went, it got all sunny and it's pretty warm now, and the girl just sort of stands there looking at me.

'Give us a sprig of that, won't you?' she says suddenly.

I ain't sure if she's talking to me, but she points at the box of plants so she must be.

I think for a minute and then I snap off a bit with flowers and give it to her.

'What's this called?' she says, putting the bit I gave her in her button hole. She's wearing a man's coat – big and warm looking.

'I've forgot,' I say. I'm never much good at names of plants and stuff. It always strikes me as funny how people can give names to plants, like they're just things or summat. When I talk to my plants I sort of call them names like Jenny or Ralph or summat – but that's my private name for them. It ain't their real name, cos how can you give a plant a name? It's funny that. I don't understand it, but it's odd like.

She squats down beside me and picks up a card from the box. 'Myosotis,' she says, then she laughs. 'Forget-me-not, and you've forgotten!'

I dunno why she's laughing, but she's got a lovely smile – sort of sunny like, and I laugh with her. Her hair's long and black like a horse's – you know, that long bit on its neck – and real shiny, so when the sun catches it, it sort of flashes like silverfoil.

'What's your name?'

'Billy.'

She looks at me hard like and I get a bit embarrassed and start making holes again. She watches me for a bit.

'D'you like this job?'

'Yeah – it's great,' I say, but I don't look at her.

The truth is, I get a bit nervous around girls and that. Some girls like Annie are OK, but big girls make me a bit nervous. There was this girl at school, Nancy, who scared me a bit. She was pretty poorly like, and couldn't speak too well, and she used to touch me and stuff. Once she pulled down her knickers and showed me her thing. I'm a bit nervous of girls on account of that.

'Where do you live, then?' she asks all of a sudden.

I point. 'In the office.'

'How did you get this job?'

I smile sort of embarrassed like. I can't remember.

'D'you reckon I could get a job here?'

I tilt my head, like I'm thinking about it, but I dunno. I wish she'd stop asking me questions. I get confused when people ask me questions.

'So how old are you, Billy boy?'

I should know the answer to that one, but all the numbers go out of my head sudden like.

'I dunno.' My face goes all red. It's stupid when you can't remember how old you are.

'You're not altogether here, are you, hen?' she says, funny like.

I tilt my head again. I get a feeling like I'm going to cry – sort of like a stone in my throat.

'Hey! Now, I'm a nosy cow, aren't I?' She says and taps me on the shoulder. 'Don't mind my questions, Billy. Just tell me to shut up.'

That makes me feel better and I look up at her. She's really got a real nice smile. Friendly like. I look at the sprig in her buttonhole. I'm glad I gave it to her.

Just then Mr Fielding comes over and I get worried he'll tell me off for giving her the flower, but he don't see it.

'Are you a friend of Billy's?' he asks the girl.

She don't stand up – she just squats there and shades the sun from her eyes with a hand. 'Yeah.'

'Well, thank God for that! You know he's been sleeping here for the past couple of days?'

'I know.'

'I didn't know what to do with him. In fact I was just thinking of getting the police. *I* can't look after him, and he can't stay here.'

'I'll take him home.' She sounds a bit tight like, and she still ain't stood up.

'He wasn't any nuisance, but I can't go on looking after him for ever you know.'

She pushes herself up using my shoulder. 'Come on, Billy boy. Get your things and we'll go.'

Her name's Marie. She says it strange, like. Ma-ree, she says. She talks with this funny accent. I think she must be a foreigner or summat. She's friendly though. She gives me a hand with my things – carrying the placky bag while I hump the suitcase. She lives quite a way from the park and I have to stop and swap arms a couple of times. I'm pretty strong and that, but that suitcase was heavy.

We finally get to her home. It's a big white building in a wide street, like it's a hotel or summat. Inside, there's a couple of bikes in the hall, and writing and drawing all over the walls. It's a good idea to draw on the walls. They didn't let us do it at school, but I think it's a pretty good idea if nobody minds.

Marie shows me her room. She's got a special key to unlock the door. There's this big red writing on the door. I suppose it says Marie or summat, but I don't ask her. Her room is real big and it's full of stuff like a shop. There's piles of clothes on the floor and this big old telly and a tailor's dummy thing and books and all sorts. She's got a little black cat – Satan, she calls it, and it miaows when we come in. It smells a bit though, her room. I think the cat has been piddling in the room – that's how it smells. Sort of like a zoo.

I'm real happy to be here, though. Marie puts on the electric fire and plugs the kettle in on the floor. Then she feeds Satan, but she don't use a plate or nothing. She just opens the tin and puts it down on the floor. Satan's still a kitten I think, and he can fit his whole head in the tin. To tell the truth, I'm a bit hungry myself, but I don't say nothing cos it ain't polite. But she gives me a cup of coffee and after I drink that I don't feel so hungry no more.

Marie talks a lot, but it's OK. It ain't like she's always asking questions like at first. She just chats and it don't matter if I don't say nothing – she just goes on. She's

34

real busy too – moving round the room and pulling open drawers and stuff. I just sit down in one of the chairs and look round the room. It's pretty interesting with all the things and that.

Then she asks me why I was living in the park and I tell her cos I couldn't stay with Mrs Riley no more. I remember taking the train and sleeping in the glass house and that, so I tell her that's what I did. Then she asks me how come I got nowhere to go, but I can't figure that one out so I pretend I'm real interested in this silvery seashell she's got. She don't ask me again, instead she just sits on her bed and shakes a little bottle and then she starts painting her toenails. We don't say nothing for a bit, and then she looks up and says I can stay in the next room for tonight. She don't show me where it is or nothing – she just says it. She says she's got a sleeping bag I can borrow.

I need to go to the toilet, so Marie shows me where it is. She has to hop over to the door, cos her toenails are still wet. She points down the hall to a red light, and says that's the toilet. I go down the hall and shut the door behind me. There ain't no window, just this red light, so it's like night time in there. I have to pull the chain a load of times before it flushes proper.

When I go back to Marie's room, she says she wants to go to sleep, so I got to go to my own room. She tells me to take my suitcase and the placky bag, and then I follow her into the next room. It ain't as big as Marie's room, and it's pretty untidy. There are these boxes and old armchairs and stuff all stacked up in a jumble. There's a mattress on the floor in the corner and Marie chucks this green sleeping bag on it.

She gives a big yawn. 'I'm going to bed now,' she says. 'You'll be all right here, won't you?' Then she gives me a smile and goes back into her room and locks the door. I know she's locked the door, cos I could hear it.

I have a proper look round the room. It's pretty dusty here, and it smells funny. To tell the truth, I don't really like it. It's OK and that, it's just a bit dusty, and I don't like that. There's a doorway that goes into the hall, but there ain't no door. I spect somebody's took it off. I go out into the hall and have a look around. There's loads of writing on the wall, but I dunno what it says. I spect it's people's names and things like that.

Marie's gone to bed, but I reckon it's pretty early for a grown-up to go to bed. It's still light and that and I don't think I've had no lunch yet. I'm pretty hungry. I wish I had some food.

I sit in one of the armchairs and jig my knee up and down for a bit. I dunno what to do now. Marie's gone to sleep, and there ain't no one else around. I can hear noises and stuff from upstairs, but no one goes past my room. I don't want to go out, just in case I get lost. I hate getting lost.

'What's up, Billy? Are you OK? Jesus Christ – I thought you were dying!'

I dunno where I am, and I sort of panic for a moment. Then I see it's Marie. My head hurts real bad and I shut my eyes.

I had a fit. I hate it when I have fits – it's scary and horrible and I always feel so poorly afterwards. The light's real bright even with my eyes shut and I have to put my arm over my face to make it dark. I'm real tired, so I just sort of lie there for a while with my arm over my face. Marie's kneeling on the floor next to me.

'You were blue!' she says. 'What happened?'

I try and sit up, but my head hurts too much, so I don't budge. I think I'm in the sleeping bag and it's night time, but I can't remember. I want to tell Marie that I had a fit, but the words won't come out. I wish she'd go away for a bit and then I'd be OK. At school if I had a fit, they'd just wait for it to go and that was it. 'Cept if it happened in class time, then I'd be allowed to go to bed and have a kip. No one worried, like. But outside they do.

I sit up after a bit. I'd forgot what the room looked like and I'm a bit surprised at first. When Marie sees me opening my eyes she asks me if I want anything. She looks tired and her make-up is a bit smudged on one eye. I tell her I'm OK, but then I see that I've made a rip in the sleeping bag. The zip thing has ripped all down one side. I try to stick the two sides together, but it's completely bust and I can't fix it. I say I'm sorry, but Marie tells me not to worry. But I feel pretty bad all the same. When I have a fit I dunno what I'm doing, and sometimes I bust things up. Once I hit Mr Browne. I don't remember it or nothing, but somebody told me after.

Marie says she'll make me some coffee, and goes back to her room. I get up and stick my trousers and trainers on. I'm still feeling a bit dizzy, and it takes me a while to do my laces up.

Marie tells me to sit in the armchair by the electric fire and gives me a mug of coffee. It's black, but I don't mind. I ask her for more sugar and she brings over the bag. I stick a load more in, till it's really sweet. Marie watches me while I drink it, like it's medicine or summat and she's a nurse.

'How often d'you get these fits?' she asks.

'Sometimes,' I say. I had one a couple of days ago, I remember that.

'Don't you have pills or something you could take?'

'I don't like pills.' This coffee tastes good, and I'm feeling better already. 'They make me feel funny.'

'How about a doctor? Shouldn't you see a doctor?'

'I'm all right now, Marie.'

She frowns and lies down on her mattress. She's still got her boots on and all. They wouldn't let us do that at school – 'no shoes on beds', that was the rule.

'Are you really working at Holland Park?' she says after a bit.

'Where's that?'

'That place you were yesterday.'

To tell the truth, it's hard to remember. I can remember the peacocks and Mr Fielding, but it seems like a long time ago.

'I don't think so,' I say in the end.

Marie pushes herself up on her elbows and sort of stares at me. She's thinking hard and don't say nothing for a long time. I look back at her for a bit, but when she don't say nothing, I finish my coffee. The sugar's like crunchy honey at the bottom and I tilt the cup until it slides down into my mouth.

'So, how d'you look after yourself then?' she asks all of a sudden.

'Beg pardon?'

'What do you do for money?'

I got some, I know that, so I feel in my trouser pockets for the coins, but I can't find none. 'I've lost it.'

'Jesus Christ, Billy!' she says. She looks annoyed or disappointed or summat. 'Who's been looking after you?'

I think about that for a bit. 'You mean Mr Jackson?'

'Who's that?'

'He's a whatnot worker. You know . . .'

'Social worker?'

'Yes.'

'And does he know where you are?' She's sitting up on the mattress now.

I look into the bottom of my mug. There's still a bit of sugar, but I can't reach it with my tongue.

'I don't think so.'

'What say?'

I shake my head. 'No,' I say louder.

I'm feeling a bit uncomfortable with all the questions and that, but Marie suddenly lies back on the bed and shuts her eyes.

I'm real hungry and I'm just thinking of asking Marie if I can have some bread or summat, when she opens her eyes and pushes herself up on her elbows again.

'So, what are you going to do? Where are you going to live?'

She looks straight at me, a bit of hair hanging across one side of her face. I dunno what to say.

'Do you want to stay here?'

'Yes, please,' I say.

'But what about your Mr Thingy? Are you going to tell him where you are?'

'I dunno.'

'Do you want Mr – '

'Jackson.'

' – hanging around you?'

'No.' Mr Jackson was all right, but he never smiles and I always feel a nuisance when he comes to see me.

Marie rolls over and picks a cigarette off the floor. She straightens it and puts it in her mouth. 'Are you signing on?' she asks out the corner of her mouth. She looks round for matches, and then leans forward and holds the fag against the electric bar of the fire. She's real close to me. I can see a tiny piece of silver paper in her hair, like a little star. She lights her fag and looks up at me. 'Well?'

She must've seen I didn't understand, cos she sighs and looks back at the fire.

Then suddenly I remember the piece of paper in my coat – the green one they gave me on the building site. I go and get it and show it to Marie.

She's quite pleased when she sees it. 'Well, at least we can get some cash for you. First thing tomorrow, we'll get ourselves to the dole office.'

She stubs her fag out and gets up. Then she sort of puts her hand round my neck. 'It's a tough old world, Billy boy. But don't you fret – if there's anyone who can beat the system, it's me.' She smiles so nice at me that I feel a lot better. I reckon Marie's pretty kind. 'Now, what about a bite to eat before I'm off?'

We have bread and sardines and another cup of coffee. I don't really like sardines so much, specially cold, but I'm so blummin hungry I eat them all up. I feel a lot better after that. When we finish, Marie sticks the plates in the sink and then she says she's got to get ready to go out.

'Give me a bit of space, now, would you, Billy?' she says.

I don't say nothing, cos I don't know what she's on about. Sometimes that happens, you know. People say things and I don't know what they mean. It's cos I'm handicapped that I don't always understand. Mr Jackson says I'll always be handicapped.

'Come on, Billy,' she says, giving my arm a bit of a tug. 'I need to get changed.'

I stand up and go back into my room. It's dark outside, but the light's on in the room, so I sit in one of the chairs and stare at the light bulb. It's like when you look at the sun and your eyes go all watery and then you shut them and you can still see a blob of light. I do that for a bit until Marie comes back in.

'Now, you'll be all right here, hen, won't you?' She's all dressed up in these nice clothes and she's got loads of make up on her face. I reckon she looks real pretty. 'I'll be back in the morning. Now no more of your fits, d'you hear?'

'All right, Marie.' I try not to have fits, but I just can't help it.

I dunno what to do now Marie's gone off. I ain't all that sleepy now, but I reckon it's bed time, cos it's been dark for ages. I carry on sitting in the chair for a bit, then I take my jeans and my trainers off and get into the sleeping bag. It's a shame I ripped it, cos now it won't zip up. I feel a bit bad for ripping Marie's sleeping bag like that, but it was cos of my fit. I hope I don't have no more fits. I hate having fits.

Marie bought me breakfast in a caff round the corner. I ate too quick at first and got hiccups and Marie laughed. She didn't eat nothing – she just smoked and looked round at the people in the caff. She knew quite a few people and one or two said hello or just nodded.

After breakfast I felt so good I couldn't stop smiling. Sometimes when I'm hungry and have a nice feed, or when I'm tired and my bed is good and warm, I get so happy I want to shout.

We walk to the bus stop and when it comes we go upstairs so Marie can smoke and I can look out the window. We go right to the front like we're the drivers. I love riding on the buses, specially on the top deck. I like looking down on top of cars and people and things. Sometimes I pretend I'm a giant – really tall and that, looking into bedroom windows and nearly banging my head on trees and lampposts and stuff.

When we get off, Marie takes me to an office and we sit down for a while until a girl comes and sees me. She gives me a form to fill out and I look at it for a bit, but I'm never much good at forms and I have to ask Marie for help. The truth is, words confuse me a bit. I can write my name and that, and I can copy pretty well, but when I try to read, the letters sort of get all jumbled up.

Anyway, Marie and the other girl fill out the form. The girl asks me a couple of questions, but they're not too difficult. Then she gives me a white card and tells me to come back on Wednesday.

We take the bus back to the house. We couldn't sit in the front this time, cos people were already there, but it was pretty good fun anyway. I prefer sitting at the front, cos then you can pretend you're the driver, but it's OK sitting at the side.

Back at the place, Marie takes me downstairs to the basement and shows me the kitchen. It's blummin huge – like the kitchen at school. There's a couple of girls by one of the stoves, chopping vegetables and stuff. One of the girls has got this bright orange hair and a ring in her nose. I never seen anyone with hair so orange, and I try not to stare, but I can't help myself. Her name's Petra. The other girl's Sonja. She's small and she's got a pointy white face like a mouse.

'They're our resident cooks. The food's not always palatable, but it's cheap, and it'll save you starving.'

'Is this a hotel, then?' I ask. I'd been thinking about it for a while. When we came back from the office I saw there was a sign over the front door like a hotel or summat.

One of the girls laughs, but she don't look up. Neither of them looked up when Marie was introducing me. 'It's not a hotel any more,' Marie says. 'We were evicted from our last squat a couple of months ago, so we moved in here. There's – ' She turns to the girl with the orange hair. 'How many of us now? Fifty?'

'Or sixty,' Petra says, chopping the onions.

'Or seventy,' Sonja laughs. She's measuring rice into a huge saucepan and when she laughs, the grains start scattering over the stove and onto the floor.

'Billy's going to be staying with me in the next room,' Marie says, munching on a bit of carrot she picked up off the table.

'Welcome to the madhouse,' Petra says. She looks up, and for a moment I think that she's crying, but it's the onions making her eyes water. She sniffs and wipes her nose on her sleeve.

'So, what are you going to surprise us with today?' Marie says.

Petra nods at the pan. 'Black eye peas.'

Marie looks in the pan. She sort of wrinkles her top lip, and then yawns. 'I'm going to bed,' she says. She puts her arm round Sonja's waist. 'Look after Billy, will you? His giro's not going to be through for a while, so let him have his food on the tab, yeah?'

'Come on, Marie,' Petra says. 'We don't know who he is.'

Marie links her other arm round Sonja's waist. 'He's a mate of mine.'

'All right. But you pay if he buggers off.'

Marie sort of snuggles her chin in to Sonja's neck and then gives her a little kiss. 'Look after him, Sonja,' she says, soft like.

Sonja looks up at me and then rubs her cheek against Marie's.

We go back to Marie's room and she switches on the electric fire. She asks me if I want to feed Satan. I say yes, but I have trouble with the tin opener, so she helps me, but I stick it on the floor and watch while Satan eats it. I really like cats. I like dogs more, but I really like cats.

Marie tells me all about this bloke who lives in the house and some other girl and summat about a motorbike. I get lost after a while, but I listen anyway. Marie's got a nice voice. She talks all funny, like she comes from another country.

Then she does summat that really surprises me. She takes her trousers off. I'm real surprised – suddenly there she is with no trousers on. I go a bit red and stare out the window so I don't see her with nothing on. But she don't get changed or nothing, she just sits on the mattress in her knickers and picks at her toenails. I try not to watch her, but it's hard not to. She's got real long legs and she's wearing these tiny pink knickers. She looks nice and that, but I'm a bit embarrassed.

Then she gets into her bed. She don't take off her top, she just gets in like she is. She talks for a bit and I just sit there by the fire and listen to her. It's nice to listen to her, even though I don't understand everything she's talking about. After a while she stops talking. I think she's asleep – she's not saying nothing or moving around or stuff.

I sit there for quite a while, just sort of looking round the room. Marie's drawn the curtains, and everything in the room looks nice and cosy. Someone knocks on the door after a while and asks if Marie's asleep. I tell him I think so, cos she ain't talked for a long time.

I try and make the cat sit on my lap, but it don't want to and jumps off. You can't make a cat do what it don't want to – it just won't do it. It ain't got a proper toilet – it goes on a piece of paper on the floor, and then sort of scratches at the carpet like it's trying to cover it up. I don't blame it. It smells like a bad fart when it goes.

It's getting pretty dark, but I just sit there feeling hungry. It ain't too bad, cos Marie left the electric fire on and I'm warm enough, but I'd like summat to eat. Just a bit of bread would do.

The room's sort of orangey on account of the electric fire. It's nice – it's like sitting by a real coal fire with nothing to do except look round and enjoy yourself.

It's ages before Marie wakes up. I think I must've been dozing as well, cos suddenly I come to when Marie says 'Who the hell – ?' a bit annoyed or scared like, and then 'Oh, it's you.'

I'm glad she's awake. To tell the truth I was getting pretty bored just sitting there. It's nice and all that to sit by a fire with nothing to do, but after a while you get bored like, and want to do summat.

Marie don't get up or nothing – she just sort of lies there. I can't see her too well, cos it's pretty dark, but I can see she's lying on her back. She's quiet for so long I think she's gone to sleep again. But then she asks me what the time is. I dunno. It's night, I know that, but I dunno what time it is. I never really got round to learning the time. Then she goes quiet again.

It's pretty hot now. I still got my coat and hat on, and I'm sitting pretty close to the fire, and I feel a bit sweaty like. I saw a film once about this steam train. It wasn't really *about* the train – the train was just sort of part of the story. Anyway, in this film there was this man driving a train and his mate was helping him – you know, sticking coal in the oven thing so it would go. The man shovelling the coal didn't have no shirt on, just a hanky round his neck, and sometimes he'd stop shovelling and wipe the sweat off his face. I forgot to say it was at night time, so it was all black outside. Anyway, it looked all hot and orangey on account of the fire. I'm just sort of reminded of that film – you know, with the heat and the orangey light and stuff.

I'm thinking so much about the train and that, I don't see Marie get up. Suddenly the light goes on and it's like I've just woken up. You know, one minute I'm in a steam train and the next I'm somewhere else. The light bulb don't have a shade and it's awful bright, so both of us just sort of squint for a while till we get used to it. Marie's hair's all over the place. She's still got her top on and she's been sweating. I can see some hair stuck to her head like sometimes babies get when they're too hot. She looks pretty ill as well. She sort of sways round a bit like she's drunk or summat, and

44

then she sits on the edge of the table. She asks me for her fags and I get up and give them to her. They're on the table next to her, but still she asks me for them. She probably didn't see them. She's still half asleep, and can't light her fag proper, so I hold the match while she sucks.

'Ta, Billy,' she says. Then she sort of lays her head on my shoulder. I'm pretty surprised like and get a bit nervy, but I don't do nothing, I just stand there fiddling with the matches. She still ain't got no trousers on and I think about Nancy and that, and how she showed me her thing once. I hope Marie ain't going to do that. It was real embarrassing.

Marie keeps dozing off on my shoulder. She's forgot about the fag, and the ash gets longer and longer till it falls off. Marie's hair's all in my face and I can smell it. It's funny, but you can smell sleep – it smells sort of warm and a bit stale like. Her hair's real shiny though. It's bloody beautiful, I reckon.

I sort of give her a nudge cos I think she's going to burn her fingers on the fag, and she straightens up. She asks me the time again. There's an alarm clock on the floor and I sort of slip away from her and hold it up so she can see it, but she tells me it's stopped.

To tell the truth, I'm blummin starved, but I don't say nothing. Marie asks me to make some coffee, so I get the kettle and go over to the sink in the corner. I know how to make coffee, and I can make tea too, but only if it's tea bags like – not if it's a tea pot and that.

After I've made the coffee Marie gets up and takes a little white envelope from a drawer and opens it up careful like. It's got this white stuff in, like salt or summat. Marie spends a long time measuring some out onto a mirror and then chops it carefully with a razor blade. Then she gets some money – a note, like – and rolls it into a tube and then sniffs the white stuff up her nose.

'D'you want some, Billy boy?'

I dunno what to say. I dunno what it is, so I just sort of shrug.

45

'No? I don't think you need it – you're speedy enough as it is.'

She folds the envelope up and sticks it back in the drawer. Then she lights another fag, even though she's got one going in the ashtray. She smokes a lot, Marie does. It ain't good for you – it makes you cough and that.

She fills the kettle again and plugs it in. She's different now – chatty like she was before. I'm worried she'll start asking questions again, but she don't. She just sort of chats about this place she went to last night. It was a sort of club or summat I think.

When the kettle boils, she pours the water in the sink and puts some cold water in. Then she turns her back on me and pulls her shirt over her head and chucks it in the corner. Blummin hell. She ain't got nothing on except her knickers. She's got her back to me, but I can still see her boobies and all. I'm real embarrassed.

'What's up, Billy?' she says, looking at me in the mirror over the sink.

'What?' I say, surprised like.

'You were making a weird noise.'

I got my hands over my eyes so I can't see.

'You're not embarrassed are you?'

I nod my head.

'Here, I'll cover myself up.' I can hear her laughing to herself, all soft and giggly. 'All right – it's safe to look now.'

I take my hands away and look at her. She's wearing a sort of long dressing gown thing – right down to her ankles. 'Better?'

I nod again. It ain't that I don't like to see her with nothing on – I *do*. It's just I get sort of worried by it. I dunno why, but I do.

Then she goes back to her washing. She spends a long time getting dressed. I can watch her this time cos she pulls her trousers and stuff on under her dressing gown, and hides behind the cupboard door when she puts her shirt on. Anyway, when she's finished, she looks bloody beautiful. She's all black and white. She's wearing these black trousers and boots, a silky white shirt and a black jacket. The jacket's made of that velvety stuff. It sort of shines like an animal's coat – a cat or summat. I love that stuff. I used to carry around a piece of that and just keep it in my pocket so sometimes I could take it out and feel it. I used to like rubbing it against my face. She looks blummin nice anyhow.

She's chatting all the time, even when she's doing her lipstick. I like listening to her. I don't really follow everything she says, but she's friendly like, and she don't mind if you don't talk back. I think if I wasn't there she'd probably just talk to Satan.

When she's finished she looks like one of them girls in the magazines – you know, all pretty and smart like. She says she's going out and says I can come too if I want, but the truth is I'm so blummin hungry I don't want to go nowhere. I don't say nothing about it, I just shake my head when she asks me if I want to go out.

Marie picks up her fags and sticks them in her pocket with her purse and then she says all sudden like, 'Oh lord! You haven't eaten anything, I suppose?'

'No, Marie.'

'Come downstairs and we'll get you some food. Bring that plate there.' She points at a plastic plate on the floor and I pick it up. She switches off the fire and then the light and shuts the door behind us. She's got a couple of keys and she locks the door.

'Why do you do that, Marie?' I ask her. We never used to lock doors at school.

'There's a lot of thieving in this place.'

It's all noisy in the kitchen. Some kids are playing with a football and they keep kicking it against the cupboards so it makes a big banging noise. Sonja and Petra are there dishing out the food. There ain't much food left in the pot.

'Hello Billy,' Sonja says. 'You're just in time.' She puts some rice on my plate and then dumps a lump of this stuff on top of it. 'Will you shut that bloody noise up!'

she shouts at the kids playing football, but they don't take no notice.

I hang around a bit watching the kids playing football while Marie chats to Sonja and Petra and then we both go upstairs again.

'You'll be all right, now?' Marie says. 'Your room's that way – ' she points along the hall. She gives me a wink and opens the front door. She don't say nothing else. I thought she might say summat more before she went, but she don't – she just shuts the door and that's it.

The light don't work in my room. I dunno if the light bulb has busted, but I can't get it to work no matter how many times I switch it on. There's a light in the hall though, so I put my plate down and drag a chair to the doorway. It's pretty dark though, and I keep banging into things before I get the chair in the right place. Then I sit down and pick up my plate. I dunno what the food is, but it ain't all that hot. There ain't no knives and forks, so I got to eat it with my fingers. I know it ain't all that polite, but I got to do it cos I ain't got no knife and fork. The food tastes pretty good though.

When I'm finished I think it's time to go to bed so I get up. It's pretty dark without the light on and I try and remember where everything is, but I still keep banging into things. I find the mattress and the sleeping bag in the corner and then I start taking my clothes off. It's pretty cold so I keep my jumper and knickers and socks on, and snuggle down. I'm blummin tired, but I lie there a bit, looking at the light patterns on the ceiling. I can hear some people laughing in another room. I'd like to talk to someone, but no one comes in, so I just lie there and think a bit. It's like being at school – lying in bed listening to noises and trying to figure out what they are, or hearing someone talk and trying to guess what they look like. I wish I was at school and Clive was in the next bed and Mr Browne was in his flat watching telly and coming round to make sure everything was OK.

*

Fullblast fell out a window a couple of years back and broke his head. He's OK now, but he still walks a bit funny. Marie told me he's a car thief – you know, he nicks cars and that.

He sometimes comes into my room and asks if he can borrow things. The first time I met him he wanted a bicycle pump. I dunno why – he don't have a bike or nothing, but anyway I didn't have one.

It's real busy living here, specially at night. There's two or three bands in the house, and sometimes it gets a bit noisy with them practising and that. I want to go and see them, but I still dunno where the noise is coming from. It's somewhere upstairs, I know that.

I ain't made too many friends yet. I ain't been here all that long and there's so many people here it's a bit like school – you know, there's too many people to remember and it takes a while to get to know them all. It's mostly pretty young people – about my age and that. But there's some older ones like Peter – that's Marie's friend. I like Peter. He used to be a gold miner – you know, he used to dig up gold from the ground. Half his teeth are gold. I know cos he showed me. He's always got lots of interesting things to show me. He's pretty old, but he ain't like a proper grown up – you know, he likes a laugh and he don't tell me off or nothing like that. Marie likes him too, and sometimes he comes to visit Marie and we sit round talking and stuff like that.

Apart from Fullblast and Peter, there's Sonja and Petra. Sometimes I go down to the kitchen to help them, cos that's where they work. Sonja's nice. She don't talk much, but she's pretty friendly. She always gives me good helpings of food, and she lets me do the washing up. She comes from some foreign country – I can't remember where. Her English ain't so good, but it don't matter much, cos she don't say much anyhow.

There ain't no baths that work in the house. There's bathrooms and that with proper sinks and baths and that, but there ain't no water, except cold. So what me and

Marie do is take shampoo and soap and stuff and go to the swimming baths and have a hot shower. We don't go swimming or nothing – we just have a shower. I like that, cos I can use this hairdrier thing on the wall, and it makes my hair all frizzy.

I usually see Marie every day. She's real friendly – she always makes sure I've ate and stuff like that, and once she took me to the laundrette so we could do our washing together. She's usually asleep for most of the day. I think she works in a nightclub or summat, cos she usually goes out at night and don't come back till I'm asleep.

If she don't go out at night, she has friends round to her room, and she invites me too. That's the best time, when I'm sitting by her fire, listening to them talk and that. One of her friends scares me a bit, though. He's called Raven, and he wears all these black clothes. Even his hair's black. He acts pretty weird sometimes – you know, one minute he'll be talking quiet like, and then he'll start shouting and being nasty to people. I dunno why he shouts and that, but I reckon he's pretty sad. That's what I reckon – you know, if someone shouts and that for no reason, then they must be pretty sad underneath. Marie don't like him much, but he still comes to see her.

I've made my room pretty nice now. I found some travel posters in the hall and Marie said I could take them, so I stuck them up on my wall. There's one of mountains with a real blue sky, and another of this castle with all these trees round it. My favourite is this one of a man and a woman sitting in a rowing boat. The man's got the paddle in his hands and the woman's sort of dipping her hand in the water, and they're smiling at each other like they're having a real good time. I like that picture. It's on the wall by my bed so I can look at it in the morning. They look real happy.

There's a big garden out the back in a sort of park-like thing. You got to have a key to unlock the gate, so I can't go in, but if I stand on a chair I can see it through my window. There ain't much to see – not many flowers and

50

stuff, but I like it anyhow. There's loads of leaves all over the grass, and nobody sweeps them up so every day there's less and less green showing. I like that.

Sometimes me and Marie and Sonja go shopping for food in the market. We go late, just when they're shutting up so we can buy the food real cheap. When Marie and Sonja buy stuff on the stalls, I go round picking up fruit and veg and stuff from the street – you know, if it ain't too bashed up and that. The last time I went I found a pineapple. It was only a bit squashed at one end and that, so we took it back with us. I was real proud of finding that, cos Marie says they cost a lot of money. I reckon Sonja's a pretty good cook. Sometimes the meals come out a bit funny, but she always gives me big helpings.

Marie ain't said nothing, but I reckon she sort of likes me. I like her – I think she's great. She don't mind me hanging round her when she's home and she always makes sure I've ate and stuff like that. I reckon Marie's real beautiful, specially when she's ready to go out at night and she's got her nice clothes and make up and stuff, or just after we've been to the swimming baths and her hair's all clean and shiny. She don't ask me to go out like she did on the first night. I dunno if I'd go cos I never been to a nightclub, but she don't ask me anyhow.

'Hey, wake up Billy!'

I dunno who it is. I got a lightbulb now, but it ain't on, so I can't see his face. Then I hear a giggle and I know it's Fullblast. Fullblast giggles a lot – high, like a girl.

I sit up and blink a bit so I can see better. 'What do you want?'

'Do you fancy coming out? Have a bit of a laugh?'

I think about that for a bit. It's nighttime and it's pretty quiet.

'No,' I say in the end. I'm warm in my sleeping bag and I want to go back to sleep.

Fullblast pulls the sleeping bag down a bit. 'Come on. We'll have some fun.'

'I don't want to.'

He don't say nothing, then he tugs at the sleeping bag again. 'Marie wants to see you.'

'Where is she?' I look at her door, but I can't see no light through the crack under her door.

'She's out.'

I can see better now. Fullblast's smiling at me, all sort of ghostly in the hall light.

'All right,' I say, and wriggle out of my sleeping bag. I get dressed as quick as I can and meet Fullblast in the hall.

'Where are we going?'

'Ladbroke Grove,' he says, zipping up his leather jacket. He looks at me and winks. 'You ready?'

The streets are real quiet – just one or two cars going by. It's weird not seeing anyone around. It's not really like night – it ain't really black. The street lights are yellowy, and it makes it look sort of like day, except it's all strange and quiet. It's pretty late I reckon, but I'm awake now and I don't feel sleepy at all.

We have to walk slow on account of Fullblast's bad leg. He's wearing a new hat, and he looks like a ship's captain or summat. He shaved his head a couple of days ago, all except for this pony-tail thing. That's why he's bought a new hat – so his head don't get too cold. I'm thinking about his hat and that, when he stops all of a sudden and asks if I can whistle. I stop and do my whistle.

'Bloody hell!' he says, putting his hands over his ears. I laugh. I'm good at whistling. I can do it with two fingers or no fingers at all. Martin Harding at school taught me to do that, and I can whistle real loud.

We carry on walking a bit till we get to a couple of shops and a pub and that. I've been here before, I think. I sort of recognise it.

'You see that chemist? I'm going in there. I want you to keep an eye out, and if you see anyone, give us a whistle. But not so fucking loud! And don't be too obvious.'

'What are you going to do?'

'What do you think, thicky? I ain't going to buy a packet

52

of johnnies now, am I?' He grins at me and then gives me a little push. 'You stand over there. And remember – not so bloody loud.'

He goes round the corner and I sit on the wall by the shop. There ain't no one around, not even any cars going by. It's blummin cold. I lost my gloves, so I stick my hands in my pockets to keep them warm.

It's interesting at night, when there's no one around. I ain't scared at night like some kids at school were. I don't mind the dark. It's being lost I don't like. It's good at night cos you can pretend you're the only person in the world and you can walk in the middle of the road and no one won't come along in a car, and you can do all sorts of things and no one won't tell you off or nothing. If you wanted, you could just do *anything*.

I get up and go round the side to see what Fullblast's up to. I can't see him nowhere, I think he must've climbed over the wall. I'm sort of standing there wondering what to do when all of a sudden, this great loud bell starts ringing. It sounds like the firebell they used to ring at school – you know, for fire practice. It scares me a bit, it's so loud. I'm looking round trying to see where it's coming from when Fullblast pops his head over the wall. He starts trying to climb over the wall, but it's pretty high, and he has trouble getting over. He looks real scared, and he's swearing to himself. Finally he makes it and sort of falls onto the pavement, and his hat falls off. He looks funny there on the ground with no hair. He sticks his hat on and starts running down the side street, then he turns and shouts back at me.

'Come on you stupid fucker – run!'

Fullblast can't run really fast on account of his bad leg, and I catch him up easy and just jog along beside him. He looks real excited. He's got a funny hoppity run, like a three-legged dog I seen once.

'What are you laughing at, you crazy bugger?'

I didn't realise I *was* laughing, but now he says it, I start laughing proper.

53

When we get to the corner, we stop running. Fullblast's out of breath, and bends over to get his breath back. His hat falls off again, so I pick it up and give it to him. He sort of snatches it back, and starts walking quick down the road.

'You're a lot of help! That's all I need – a moron with the giggles!'

He looks like he's angry, but I can tell he's not really. He stops under a street light and takes some stuff out of his pocket and looks at it. Then *he* starts giggling. 'A bottle of eyedrops and some throat sweets! Not bad for a night's work!'

He opens the packet of sweets and pours them all out into his hand. He gives me a pile and chucks the packet away. I try one of the sweets. They ain't too bad – they taste sort of blackcurranty. Fullblast stuffs the whole lot into his mouth.

'Eyedrops?' he says, his voice all muffled with the sweets. 'I wonder if you can get a buzz off this stuff? You can from nose drops.'

He looks at the writing on the side of the bottle. His mouth is full of sweets and he starts coughing – one or two sweets shooting out his mouth like popcorn. 'Ah, fuck it!' he laughs.

He takes aim at a car on the other side of the street and bounces the bottle across the road, like skimming a stone across water. The bottle misses the car and bounces off a wall, but it don't smash. It must be pretty hard glass.

Marie's door's open when we get back, and when she hears us come in, she sticks her head round the door.

'Where've you been, Billy?'

'Out with Fullblast.'

She comes into my room and looks at me, and then at Fullblast. Fullblast takes off his hat and pulls a funny face at me.

'What've you been up to? You haven't been thieving, have you?'

'No – course not,' Fullblast says all sarcastic like.

'You have, haven't you!' She looks real angry. 'Fucking hell, Fullblast! You can get busted if you want, but leave Billy out of it. He's only a – '

She stops and looks at me, and then back at Fullblast. 'He doesn't know what he's doing.'

'We got fuck-all anyway. Waste of time.'

She points at Fullblast. Her eyes are real black. 'You try anything like that again and I'll – '

'You'll?' Fullblast's got his hands on his hips, like a woman. He squeezes his lips together like he's going to kiss Marie.

She turns away from him. 'Bugger off, Fullblast.'

He sticks his hat back on at a funny angle. 'Rather you than me, lover boy,' he says, giving me a wink.

Marie spins round like somebody's pulled her. 'What does *that* mean?'

'He's hot for you, Marie baby. Billy boy here wants to get into your pants – anyone can see that.'

'You – ' She looks round for summat to throw at Fullblast, but he laughs and nips out the door.

'Bastard,' she shouts.

I go and sit on my bed and watch Marie. She's still dressed, but she ain't got no shoes on. Her toenails need painting.

'Bastard,' she says again.

'Don't worry, Marie.'

'Don't worry? You're going to get yourself into trouble hanging round that crazy bastard.'

'He's all right, Marie,' I say, quiet like.

'No, he's not!' She's angry at *me* now. 'He's a fucking nutcase!'

'Like me?'

She catches her breath like she's stubbed her toe or summat. 'Who told you that?' she asks after a minute.

'Everybody.'

'You're not a – ' She shakes her head. 'You mustn't believe that.'

I shrug and lie down on the bed. I'm pretty tired now

I'm in the warm. Marie looks at me. She looks pretty worried.

'Billy, you mustn't think that.'

'I had fun with Fullblast. Why did you tell me off?'

She sits down on the edge of the bed and fiddles with the zip of the sleeping bag.

'Someone's got to look after you.'

I start crying. I don't want to, but I can't stop myself. I roll over so Marie can't see me.

'What's up, hen?'

I don't say nothing. I dunno why I'm crying – I just feel sort of sad. I had a good time with Fullblast and then Marie don't understand, and I dunno, but it makes me feel sad. Sometimes it's hard when people don't understand.

Ibrahim's got a video and sometimes he lets me watch it. I can't always follow the story in films and that, but sometimes I like watching the telly – specially nature programmes and that. He never opens his curtains, so it's always like night in his room, even if it's daytime. He's got this red light, so it looks all cosy, and sometimes he uses a candle. It's pretty cosy, but to tell the truth it ain't all that comfy. All he's got is a mattress on the floor and this video machine. There ain't no chairs or carpet or nothing, so if I go and see him I have to sit on the floor. I don't mind it really.

I don't think people in the house like Ibrahim all that much. I can tell by the way people look at him. He don't talk too much cos his English ain't so good, so people don't really bother to talk back. But sometimes they come to his room to watch the video. He don't mind that at all – I think he likes the company. When he shows a film or summat his room's like a little cinema – you know, people sitting round watching the telly in the dark, and smoking and laughing at the funny bits and that.

When it's just me and Ibrahim he talks a lot about his home. I can't remember where he comes from, but it's in the desert I think. I reckon he's pretty homesick to tell the truth. When it's just me and him he plays his favourite video and stops it when it comes to a picture of a town where he lived. It looks pretty nice from the pictures. All hot and that. It must be blummin cold in England if you come from the desert.

He's got a wife in his home, but he ain't seen her for ages. I reckon that must be pretty lonely like, not ever seeing your family. He says he wants to go back to his country, but he can't. I dunno why, but he says he can't.

Sometimes he talks in a foreign language – you know, just to himself like. I don't understand it or nothing, but I like listening anyhow. It's like sort of music.

He's got a friend – this black man who comes to the house sometimes. I don't think he lives here, cos I never see him except in Ibrahim's room. He usually brings food and stuff, but he don't stay for long. He just brings stuff for Ibrahim and then goes. Ibrahim never goes out, not even to the shops or nothing. I spect it's cos it's too cold. I reckon it must be real cold after the desert. When his friend comes, they talk together in this foreign language. I suppose he's from Ibrahim's country, but I never asked.

Nobody likes Ibrahim much. Nobody goes to see him unless he's showing a video. But I think Ibrahim's OK. To tell the truth, I think he's pretty lonely on account of his wife and that. He's always pleased to see me and sometimes he gives me food and stuff. Once he told me he likes me cos I don't ask questions.

I think Ibrahim must be ill or summat, cos Marie says he's a junky – you know, he's got to take drugs and stuff like that. It's a shame really that people got to take medicine. But they have, you know, or else they'll get iller. But I think Ibrahim's OK. He's a little funny sometimes, but he's real kind and that.

If the weather's all right and it's not raining or nothing, I usually go to the garden to help Mr Frost. He's got a key, and if he's in the garden he lets me in. It's not his job or nothing, but he likes doing stuff in the garden, and most days he's there. He's pretty old and don't hear too well, and I have to shout so he can hear me. There was a boy at school who was deaf, but he could read lips so we didn't have to shout. But I do with Mr Frost. He's always saying 'What say, boy?' and I have to go right up to him and shout. I think he should get a hearing aid – it's easier than shouting all the time.

We don't do much in the garden – a bit of weeding or raking leaves and that, but I like it anyhow. Nothing much grows in winter, but it's nice to be in the garden. Mr Frost says it looks real nice in the summer when all the flowers come out. I can't wait for the summer. I bet it looks real good.

Marie helps me with my money, and every week she gives me some so I can buy plants and stuff for my room. I got loads of plants now. I dunno their names and stuff, but they're real nice. There's this flower shop not far from the house, and I go there and buy summat every week. I go on my own like, not with no one else. I reckon that's pretty grown up. The woman in the shop's pretty friendly and she tells me what to do with the plants – you know, water them once a week, or keep them out of draughts and that. The other week she tried to get me to buy some different plants, but I didn't do it. I get the same plants every week – these real nice ones with the soft petals. I got loads of them now – mostly different colours. I really like them ones. They're my favourite. Fullblast calls me Billy Weed on account of all my plants. I told him they ain't weeds, but proper plants like, but he still keeps on calling me Billy Weed.

I promised Marie I wouldn't go out with Fullblast again. She said I'd get into trouble if I did. She said Fullblast nicks things, and if I did that, the police would come and take me away. So I promised I wouldn't go out with him again. I wouldn't nick things anyhow, cos it's wrong.

I reckon of all my favourite bits, I like when me and Marie are on our own best. Like when we go to the laundrette, or she takes me to the swimming baths to have a hot shower.

It's OK when all the others are round, but it's best when it's just her and me.

Marie works in this place most nights, so she don't usually come home till I'm asleep. I dunno what her job is cos she never told me. I think it's working in this club or summat. She don't really like it, but she does it anyway. I spect she can't get another job or summat.

If I'm with Ibrahim, I go to bed when he tells me, otherwise I just go to bed when I'm tired. It's pretty noisy at night-time, specially if there's a band practising in the house. I don't mind it, but it's pretty hard going to sleep with this banging going on. I like having lots of people round the house – it's like school. It's just at night it gets a bit noisy.

One night I'm in bed – just sort of lying there, thinking about stuff and that when Marie walks in and goes straight over to her door. It's dark, but I know it's Marie cos she's got her jangly boots on and I can hear them.

'Marie?' I say. I'm pleased to have her back so early. Like I say, she don't usually come back till the morning.

She don't hear me, so I say it again, but she just unlocks the door and goes into her room.

I dunno why, but I get the feeling's summat's up – you know, a sort of scared feeling in my tummy. So I get out of bed and stick some clothes on. I can see the light under Marie's door, but there's no noise or nothing. She usually plays music when she's home.

I knock on her door, but she don't say nothing, so I just push it open.

'Go away, Billy.'

She's lying on her mattress with her face in the pillow. She's still got her boots on, and they're a bit muddy.

I dunno what to do, so I just sort of stand there. Satan's miaowing for food but I don't pay it no attention. Summat's up with Marie – I can tell. I sort of kneel down and give her a touch on the shoulder. She jumps a bit, but she don't look up. Her face is still stuck in the pillow.

'Leave me, Billy.'

'What's wrong?'

'Just go away.'

She starts crying now. She don't make no noise, but I know she's crying. She's sort of shaking like you do when you laugh.

I dunno what to do. I hate it when people cry, cos it makes me want to do the same thing. I sort of get this lump in my throat and then my eyes start to sting.

I'm sort of kneeling there, so I put my hand on Marie's back to make her feel better, but she rolls away from me.

'Don't touch me.'

Then I see her face. I can't believe it. One eye's all red and swelled up and her lip's been split. It's all puffy and bloody. I stare at her, then I start crying.

She's so beautiful, and why did this happen? I can't get any words out. We just look at each other – me crying and Marie just staring. She looks like someone else. She don't look like Marie at all.

I try and stop my crying, but every time I look at her it starts again. I can't understand why she looks like this. She's so pretty normally, but now she's all bloody and hurt.

'Get me a cigarette, Billy,' she says. Her words come out funny – sort of muffled like, cos of her lips.

I get up and have a look round the room, but things are blurry on account of my tears and I can't find her fags. I sort of rub my face with my hands and have a proper look, but I can't find none. I'm real confused.

'I've got one,' she says.

Marie's sitting up on the bed with a packet of fags. She looks pretty calm now. She ain't crying or nothing, but her face is horrible to look at. I find her some matches and try and light one, but it won't light. She takes them off me.

'Sit over there, will you hen?' she says, pointing to the chair by the fire.

I go and sit down. I stopped crying now, but I feel a bit shaky so I look down at my feet and try to figure things out. That's what I do when I get worried – I try to figure it out. But I can't do it – all I can think about is Marie's face.

'What happened, Marie?' My voice goes all funny, but I keep from crying.

She don't say nothing – she just shakes her head. Satan comes over and rubs against her hand like he does when he's hungry, but she just stares at him.

'Boil me some water, will you Billy?'

I find the kettle and plug it in. Marie looks calm now, but she's all tight in her body, like she's real angry and she's trying not to show it.

'They said they'd kill me,' she whispered. She shuts her eyes and sort of lets out a moan like a dog whining or summat.

She's still got the fag and matches in her hands, so I take them away from her. Then I sort of hold her hands tight while she rocks back and forward on the bed. Her moan gets louder and she opens her mouth till she's bawling like a baby. It scares me a bit, but I still hold onto her hands. She's rocking real hard now – her eyes shut and her mouth open, her face all bashed up.

I get an idea to hug her, so that's what I do, and we rock back and forward together. She hangs onto me real hard like she's scared I'll let go, making this funny noise. To tell the truth, it's pretty scary.

We hang onto each other for ages, not saying nothing. My legs get all tingly after a bit on account of how I'm sitting, but I don't move. I just stay there holding onto Marie.

I sort of give her hair a stroke and say 'there, there' like I seen people do with babies. She stops her moaning after a bit. The kettle's boiling like mad so I get up careful like and unplug it.

Marie's still rocking – hugging herself like some of the poorly kids at school used to. She looks a bit cold, so I go and fetch the blanket off my bed and wrap it round her shoulders. She don't seem to notice – she don't say thank you or nothing. She just stares at the floor and rocks.

Her face is pretty bloody and that, so what I do is wet some paper tissues under the tap, and real careful like,

I rub the blood off of her mouth and chin. She sort of flinches, but I dab real soft and she lets me finish. Her bottom lip is fat and purple and there's a split down the middle. Her eye ain't bleeding, but it's almost closed up. I don't touch it cos it looks too painful.

Marie's face is real white and she's still sort of staring like she don't know what's going on. Then she pushes the blanket off and stands up. She pours the hot water into the sink.

'Leave me for a bit, Billy,' she says with her back to me, so I go out and sit on my bed. I'm pretty worried to tell the truth. I ain't never seen Marie like this. It ain't just her face being all bashed up and that – it's the way she didn't say nothing, but just stared at the floor. Normally she's real happy. Summat bad's happened to her.

I wait till her room's quiet, then I tap on the door and go in. She's in bed now, lying on her back and staring at the ceiling. I go and sit on the floor by the mattress and watch her. We don't say nothing for a long time.

'It was horrible,' she says at last. She puts her hand out without looking at me, and I take hold of it.

'They were so . . . vicious.' She looks at me like she's asked a question and she wants me to answer. Her hand's gone all limp, then she suddenly takes it away.

'Why, Billy? Why do you hate us so much?'

I dunno what to say. I dunno what she's going on about, so I don't say nothing. She's real upset about summat – I know that, but *I* don't hate her. I bite my lip. I wish she wouldn't look at me like that – she's gone all hard and like she don't like me no more.

I feel her touch my hand again, but I can't look at her. I feel all upset now. Marie's my friend. I don't hate her.

'I'm sorry, Billy. Don't cry – it wasn't your fault.'

It's like a dream. Everything was OK. I was lying in bed, happy, and then Marie comes home and she's all bashed up, then she says I hate her. I can't look at her, so I go and fetch a tissue and wipe my nose. I dunno why I'm crying. It's silly to cry, specially when it ain't me who's hurt, but

I can't stop. I'm really unhappy. I can't remember being so unhappy – not ever.

I go back and sit down again, and she takes a hold of my hand and squeezes it like she's saying sorry or summat. I still don't understand.

'Why did they hit you, Marie?'

'They're animals – that's why.'

'But why?'

I look at her, but she just shakes her head.

She lies there for a long time, not saying nothing. Then she asks me to get a small bottle of pills from her drawer. I find them easy enough, and give her the bottle. It's a little brown bottle like the ones they used to have at school. She swallows a couple of the pills and lies back down again. Her hair's all over the pillow, and I want to brush it. Looking at her hair, I can pretend her face ain't all hurt and that, and that everything's OK and that. But she starts crying again.

I sort of sit by her bed till she falls asleep. It's weird, but when she's asleep she looks real young, even though her face is all puffy. I'm not tired no more so I just sit and watch her. I still don't understand why she was all bashed up. She's my friend.

I been to hospital once to visit someone. I can't remember who, but they were pretty poorly like and all round the bed was flowers and fruit and that. I remember cos it looked so nice. Sitting there, I think about that for a while, then I decide to bring all my plants in and stick them round the bed. I don't have no fruit, but I reckon just plants are OK without the fruit. So that's what I do – I bring all my plants and the flowers Mr Frost gave me a couple of days ago. It was nice of Mr Frost to do that. He gave me a whole bunch of flowers for nothing. I stuck them in a milk bottle cos I ain't got a proper flower vase, but they look OK like that I reckon. When I finish putting them all round the bed, it looks real nice. I reckon Marie'll be pretty surprised when she wakes up. I hope it makes her feel better.

It's pretty late, but I don't go to bed. What I do is sit in the chair by the fire. I reckon if Marie was awake, she'd like the company – you know, so she wouldn't be afraid or nothing. So I stay there just in case she wakes up.

Marie's pretty under the weather for the next couple of days. It's not just her face and that, though it looks pretty painful still. It's like she's real sad and quiet like. I been spending a lot of time with her these days. It's nice for me, even though she's sad. She don't want to be on her own, even at night, so what I done was drag my mattress and sleeping bag into her room, and that's where I'm sleeping now – on her floor. She don't sleep too well, and she gets bad dreams even though she takes pills and that to help her sleep.

The day after her accident we went to the swimming baths so she could have a shower. We go once or twice a day now. All Marie wants to do is wash. I don't mind going with her. I just hang round the entrance and wait for her. Marie told me she'd teach me to swim one day. I'd like that.

She don't go to work no more, and sometimes she cries for no reason. I do my best to make her feel better, but still she cries and that. She likes the flowers and plants in her room, so I left them there.

I feel real sorry for Marie. It ain't nice what happened to her. Sonja helps me look after Marie, but mostly it's me, cos Sonja's pretty busy in the kitchen. I reckon Marie likes me being round her, and doing things for her. I usually make her coffee, and if she runs out of fags or needs summat from the shops, I go for her. I don't mind doing that. I reckon Marie's the best friend I ever had.

I introduced Marie to Mr Frost, and sometimes if she wants to go out and get some fresh air, we go to the gardens. I think she likes the gardens. She don't help out or nothing – she just sits on the bench, or wanders round looking at things, but I think she likes it. To tell the truth, there ain't much to do in the garden, but we go quite a lot anyhow. Mr Frost's nearly always there, and if he is, he unlocks the gates and lets us in.

The weather's pretty nice these days. It's still real cold, but the sky's clear and sunny. I like days like that – they smell real good. I just wish Marie wasn't so sad.

I like Marie – I really do. I had a girlfriend at school – Sara, her name was. She wasn't a proper girlfriend or nothing – we was just mates like. But I called her my girlfriend, and it made me feel pretty good. She had summat growing in her brain and she died. That really upset me, that did. I visited her a couple of times in the hospital, and then Mr Browne told me she died. Just like that. That made me real sad, cos she was my best girlfriend. Sometimes I think about her, and that makes me feel all sad when I remember her, cos she's dead now.

I reckon Marie's my best friend now. She ain't exactly my girlfriend, but we spend loads of time together, going out and that. I ain't asked her if she's my girlfriend, but I think she is in a way. I know she likes me cos she told me.

The things I like best about Marie are how she laughs and her hair. She lets me brush her hair sometimes. I love doing that. It's long and shiny and it takes me ages to do it. It's a blummin beautiful colour – all sort of black with bits of brown in it, and sometimes, in the sun, it looks sort of blue.

It's OK living with Marie. At first I got a bit embarrassed – you know, about taking off my clothes and that, but now it's OK. I go and change in the toilet and wear my mac like a dressing gown, and then hop into my sleeping bag and take it off. Marie gets changed behind the wardrobe door, and anyway, I always shut my eyes when I know Marie's getting undressed.

Like I say, Marie don't work no more, so we have the whole day together if we want. Sometimes she wants to do things on her own, but most times we do things together – you know, like going to the swimming baths or going shopping and stuff like that. I really like doing things together. It makes me feel all grown up, like Marie's my girlfriend and that.

I reckon Marie is really pretty – prettier than Sara. Sara had summat wrong with her eyes, and to tell the truth, she wasn't pretty at all. But she had nice hair – not so long as Marie's, but just as shiny. It was sort of orangey, not black like Marie's, but it was real nice too. I never brushed it or nothing like I do to Marie's. They didn't like us touching the girls at school, so I wasn't allowed. When I brush Marie's hair in the morning, I sometimes think about Sara. I reckon if Sara's in heaven, she wouldn't mind me brushing someone else's hair. There's nothing wrong with being friends – it's only when you do summat selfish it's wrong.

To tell the truth, I get a bit jealous of the other people who come and see Marie. She ain't got a boyfriend or nothing – not a proper one, but still a lot of boys come and see her. I don't think she's all that keen on them, and sometimes she kicks them all out, if it's getting late and she wants to go to bed. She likes Peter, I know that. I like Peter too. He's pretty old, but he's real nice. He was real kind to Marie after her accident. He spent a long time with her, talking, and making her feel better when she was crying and that. Peter's pretty nice, but to tell the truth I like to be with Marie on my own best. When she's with other people I don't always understand what they're going on about and that makes me feel stupid. Still, I don't think Marie likes any of the boys much – except for Peter. I can tell by the way she looks at them. I know Marie likes me cos she told me. I ain't sure if I'm her boyfriend or not.

She's better now, you know, after her accident and that. Her face is all healed up, and she don't cry so much. She still gets a bit funny sometimes, and won't go out at night, even if there's a party or summat. That suits me, cos I like to stay in with her. It's great when it's just me and her in the evening. What we do is, pull the curtains shut and switch on the fire. Then Marie'll put a record on, or sometimes the radio, and we just sit about chatting. Marie likes to ask me about my family and that, but I don't really like talking about that much – except Annie, that is.

Sometimes Marie writes some stuff – poems and that, or else she reads a book. She likes reading. If she does that, I get on with the jigsaw. Marie bought me this blummin huge jigsaw with millions of bits. It's a picture of a load of boats in the water. It's real difficult on account of all the sea and sky and that, but it's real fun. I'm good at jigsaws – I'm twice as quick as Marie.

Marie read me one of her poems the other day. It was called 'Billy Bayswater' and she said it was about me. I didn't understand it all, but I thought it was real beautiful. There was summat about my head in the stars and walking on clouds in it. I liked that bit, I did. Walking on clouds.

I don't see much of Fullblast now. To tell the truth, I'm a bit sad about Fullblast. When he heard about Marie's accident he just made a joke. That upset me, that did. I don't think it was right to make a joke about that. I like to have a laugh and that, but there's some things you shouldn't laugh at. Like when someone gets hurt.

Ibrahim's gone now. He got in trouble last week and he's in prison. It's a shame really, cos Ibrahim was OK. He sold his video, and so nobody went to see him no more, except for me. And then he got arrested for summat, and now he's in prison. Carl from upstairs got arrested too, and he said that Ibrahim was screaming all night in the room next to him in the prison, and when they opened the door in the morning, he'd scratched all the skin off of his face. I dunno why he did that, but when I heard Marie tell that, I felt really horrible. I dunno why anybody would do that. Now I don't suppose he'll never get to his home and see his wife again.

Marie's teaching me to swim. I bought a pass for the swimming baths so I can get in for free. I had to take my picture in one of them photo booths. That was fun, that was. I took two of me and two of me and Marie. In the ones with both of us, we was laughing like mad. They're real nice pictures – I keep them in my pocket and take them out sometimes to look at them. We look real happy in them.

It ain't like I'm scared, but to tell the truth, swimming's a lot harder than I thought. I don't mind getting wet and that – I don't even mind my head going under water. That's OK, except when I get water up my nose. It's the floating bit that's difficult. I can do it OK if I hang onto the side, but when I let go I just sink. Marie's real patient though, and she tries again and again. It's pretty good fun, but it'd be better if I could float. Marie says I got to relax more. I said I'll try.

Marie's a brilliant swimmer. I like watching her going up and down the baths. I usually stand at the shallow end after she's finished teaching me the floating bit, and watch her have her swim. She ain't so quick as some of the others, but she's real good at swimming. She don't hardly splash at all. She's like one of them underwater swimmers I seen on telly – you know, all slow and graceful like.

The first time we went, Marie wore her bra and knickers, but she was told off for that, so she bought this real nice swimming costume. It's all shiny and blue, and it's real tight. I try not to look, but you can see her boobies and that. She looks blummin beautiful in that swimming costume.

We go to the baths a lot still. Not every day like we used to just after her accident, but quite a lot all the same. To tell the truth, my favourite bit is having a hot shower afterwards. But Marie likes swimming, so I don't mind going with her. She says it's ages since she's done any exercise, and it's good for her. She says we'll get some old bikes so we can bike to the baths instead of walking. That's a good idea, I reckon. I used to have a bike before I went to school. That was ages ago – I hope I ain't forgot how to ride one.

I'm still sleeping on Marie's floor. I hope she don't tell me to go back to my old room, cos I really like sleeping with Marie. The best bit's when the light's out, and I can listen to her breathing, and if I want to say summat – you know, summat that happened in the day – I can just speak soft and she'll hear me. I don't even mind if she's asleep and she don't answer, it's just as good listening to her breathing. She's sleeping much better now, and she don't have to take pills no more. I'm glad about that, cos to tell the truth, she used to get a bit strange sometimes after she took them. You know, sort of clumsy and sleepy like she was drunk or summat. Anyway, she's stopped taking them, so she's back to normal.

The other best bit about sleeping with Marie is waking up and seeing if she's awake. Sometimes she is, and sometimes she ain't. Like I say, she's sleeping well now, and she's often up before I even wake up. But even if she's up, she ain't dressed properly – she just wears her dressing gown. She don't get dressed till after she's had her cup of tea, and that's my job to make it. As soon as I'm awake, I stick the kettle on and make us two cups of tea.

'Thank you, William,' Marie says to me when I give her the tea, and I say 'Is there anything else, your Highness?' like we're king and queen or summat. Then she gets back into bed, dressing gown and all, and I hop back into my sleeping bag and we drink our tea.

We never open the curtains till after breakfast and we're dressed. Marie keeps cornflakes and stuff in the room, and if there's any milk we have that, or else we have some toast and jam. After breakfast, I go out to the toilet and get dressed and Marie gets dressed in the room. Then she'll open the curtains and look out to see what the weather's like, and then she'll say summat like 'How about a walk, Billy?' or 'Jigsaw weather today, hen.'

Like I said, I reckon Marie's the best friend I ever had.

'Billy, it's about time we did something about the way you look.'

Marie's standing behind me and we're both looking in the mirror on the inside of the wardrobe. She reaches over and brushes the hair off of my eyes.

'You could use a haircut.'

She brushes my hair behind my ears and holds the top

bit to one side. It's ages since I had a haircut. We used to have them real often at school.

'How about we cut the sides and front short, and leave the back long?'

'OK,' I say. I don't really mind. I love Marie touching me like she's doing now. Her hands are real soft and warm and when she touches me, I feel all sleepy and happy. To tell the truth, I couldn't care less about my hair. All I want is her to carry on brushing my hair with her hands.

She puts her hands on my shoulders and steers me to the chair. 'You sit down and wrap this towel round your neck.'

She chucks a bath towel to me. 'And I'll borrow Sonja's scissors.'

I do like she says, and sit there with the damp towel round my neck and wait for her to come back.

It's real quiet in the morning – there ain't hardly anyone moving about the house. I like it when it's quiet and it's just me and Marie. It's like we're sort of living here together – you know, sort of like we're married or summat and living in a proper house of our own and all that.

It's good and sunny today and everything in the room's all lit up and interesting looking. My plants look real healthy in the sun and the photos Marie's stuck on the wall are all shiny. She's always sticking piccys on the wall – you know, things she cuts out of mags and that.

Marie comes back in and gives me a smile. She's real happy nowadays. I'm really really glad about that. I hate to see someone sad.

'Now, sir,' she says, walking round the chair and looking at me like she's a real barber. 'A short back and sides was it? Or a mohican?'

I laugh, but I dunno what to say so I just shrug. Marie starts combing my hair. There's a few knots in it and it hurts a bit when she tugs the comb, but I don't say nothing. It's just great to have Marie touching me like this.

When she's finished combing, she puts the mirror on the table in front of me so I can see myself.

'Completely off the ear I think, don't you?' she asks, holding my hair back. I turn my head sideways to see how I look with my ears showing, but I can't see proper.

'It makes you look quite distinguished.'

'What do you mean?' I turn the other way, but it's difficult to see in the mirror cos the corner's been broke off.

'Older,' she says.

We had real fun with Marie cutting my hair. She took her time, and done it real careful. I couldn't really see what she was doing, but I didn't mind. I trust Marie – I think she's really great.

When she's done, she hands me the mirror and I have a look. I must admit I'm a bit shocked at first. She's cut it real short, so it feels all bristly when I rub my hands over it. But I reckon it looks OK. It's always a shock when summat's different, but you get used to it in the end.

She takes the towel off me and then squats down and begins brushing bits of hair off of my face with her fingers. It's real lovely to have Marie there so close to me with her brushing her fingers over my face. She ain't really looking at my face, but straight into my eyes.

'You're a handsome devil – you know that, Billy?'

She lifts her eyebrows at me and then stands up and goes over to the sink. I give a laugh.

'You don't believe me?' she says, turning the tap on.

I carry on laughing. I'm laughing cos I'm so happy. Marie's filling the kettle with water and Satan's sleeping on the windowsill and the house is quiet and Marie says I'm handsome. I don't think I ever been so happy.

Marie smokes a fag while I brush up the hair and stick it in the bin. I wish Marie was still cutting my hair. I really liked it, the way she moved my head and brushed her fingers through my hair.

She's lying on the bed, blowing smoke at the ceiling. The smoke sort of hangs in blue layers above the bed and I watch it for a bit. Someone upstairs is playing a record – I can just make out the thumping of the drum.

71

'Let's go out, Billy,' Marie says all of a sudden. 'Get you some new clothes.'

She rolls off the bed and stubs the fag out. Marie gets all excited when she gets a good idea – suddenly she's all full of energy and she can't sit still. She's like that now – her eyes are all bright and shiny in the sun.

'We'll go to the charity shop and see what they've got.'

There's a charity shop on the main road where sometimes me and Marie go. She bought herself a pair of shoes there once. They weren't new or nothing, but they looked OK. I've forgot what they're like, but they were pretty good, I remember that.

It's cold outside, even with my hat pulled over my ears. I tell Marie I'd like some gloves cos I lost mine, and she says we'll have a look and see if there's any good cheap ones. I like going shopping with Marie, even if we don't buy nothing. I just like looking in shop windows.

The charity shop's not really a proper shop – it ain't smart or none of that, and there's just a couple of old women sitting by an electric fire and helping out customers when they want to try on clothes and that. It's pretty scruffy and it's got this funny smell – sort of dusty like. But it's interesting enough. There's loads of stuff – you know, bits and pieces like old clothes and teapots and books and that. The first thing Marie does when she goes in is go over to the hats. I knew she'd do that, cos she really likes hats. She's got loads in her room.

'Come over here, Billy. Try this on.'

She's holding up this straw hat – a bit like the one in the picture on my wall – you know, the one with the man in the boat. I take off my woolly hat and try it on. It feels funny after my other hat. It's all hard and cold, but Marie laughs and turns me round so she can see it from all sides.

'It's perfect! Have a look in the mirror.'

I go over to the long mirror and have a look. I reckon it looks really great. It's a bit bust on one side but I really like it. It makes me look all grown up – you know, like someone in a film or summat.

'We'll need a jacket to go with that,' Marie says. She's looking through this rack of suits so I go and give her a hand. There's this white blazer with these thick purple stripes, and I take it off the hanger. We both look at it for a bit. I ain't sure if I like it. It's sort of more like a pyjama top than a blazer.

'I dare you, Billy.'

I think about it for a bit. 'OK.'

Marie helps me off with my coat and holds it while I slip the jacket on. It's pretty big, even with my jumper underneath, but it's got this lovely silky lining and it feels really comfy.

Marie steps back and sort of squints at me. 'Hmm . . .'

We both go over to the mirror and look at it.

'Hmm . . .' I say this time. It sort of looks OK, but not quite.

Marie steps in front of me and rolls the sleeves up to my elbows and then turns the collar up. She squints at me again and then looks round the shop for summat.

'Ah!' she says, and then goes over to the other side of the shop. I have another look at myself in the mirror. It ain't too bad. I push the hat back and then stick my hands in my pockets. I try and keep a straight face, but I can't help grinning at myself. Marie said I was a handsome devil!

'How about this?' She drapes this green scarf round my neck. It's real cold against my skin and I jump a bit, but I reckon it looks really good. It's nice material – all heavy and silky like. It looks great with the jacket and hat.

'Turn round, Billy. Let's have a look.'

I do a little turn like I seen them fashion models do. Marie watches me a bit then she nods her head. 'You look great, hen.'

I grin at myself in the mirror. I look like someone else – you know, some famous person like.

'Are you going to get summat, Marie?' I say.

She's looking through the dress rail. 'I can't really afford to, but what the hell!'

73

She picks up this blue skirt and holds it against her legs and then puts it back on the rail.

'You're only young once, Billy boy. You might as well enjoy it.'

She takes out this dark red dress with these big white dots and goes over to the mirror. She smoothes the dress out against her front and looks at it in the mirror.

Standing there with her back to me, she looks more beautiful than I ever seen her. I get this real strong urge to stand behind her and put my arms round her and give her a hug, but I don't move. I just stand there watching her with her hair falling out of her hat, holding this dress against herself.

'What do you think, Billy?'

She turns round to face me.

It's a pretty dress I suppose, but anything would look pretty on Marie.

'Well?' she asks.

I can't think of nothing to say, so I just nod. She looks blummin beautiful, that's all I know.

Marie asks one of the old women if she can use the changing room, and she shows her where it is. I have a look round the shop while Marie gets changed. There's a nice china dog on the side by some books, but I don't go over and have a look. Normally I would, but I just don't want to move. I can feel this happy feeling bubbling in my tummy. When I get like that, I get my urge to shout. That's all I want to do – I just want to shout and jump. I make myself breathe slow. I get too excited sometimes and spoil things. I don't want to be sick or nothing. That would make Marie disappointed.

I look over at the changing room. There's a curtain across the door, but it ain't long enough so I can see Marie's feet and her black trousers all in a ball on the ground.

I can't wait for Marie to be finished here so we can walk down the street in our new clothes. Sometimes she holds onto my arm in the street – you know, just natural, like I'm a girl and she's just a friend or summat. I get real proud when she does that. Marie's so pretty and lovely, I want everyone to see us, so they'll say how grown up and lucky I am to have such a lovely girlfriend.

Marie pulls the curtains back and steps out. She's got the dress on and she's taken her hat off so her hair's all over her shoulders. I can see her little gold necklace twinkling like a star round her neck.

The old woman from the shop asks her if it fits and Marie does a couple of turns in front of the mirror.

'Pretty well.'

She stops turning so she's facing me. 'D'you like it?'

I look at the dress. It's got these tight sleeves that look too short and the bottom bit is all bunched up so when she turns it all billows out. The waist is real narrow – there's a little belt there that Marie tied up. Her neck and shoulders are bare and cold looking. It's a beautiful dress. She looks so pretty.

'I think it's great.'

'Not too loud?'

She sees I don't understand. 'Bright,' she says.

I shake my head.

'I'll take it,' she says to the old woman. 'And what Billy's wearing too.'

I want to keep my new clothes on, so the old woman gives me a big paper carrier bag to put my mac and woolly hat in. Marie sticks her jeans in too – she's going to wear the dress under her coat. Marie pays the woman and we go out.

Marie's in a real good mood – she likes buying things. She grabs a hold of my arm and skips along beside me. She keeps poking me in the side with every step.

'Come on – skip!'

I try doing it, but I get sort of tangled up.

'You're *hopping*. Skip. Like this.' She skips on ahead of me, and then turns round. 'See?'

I try it. It's blummin difficult. I nearly get it right, but I end up hopping again. We both laugh and Marie takes hold of my arm again.

'Let's forget that,' she says.

We take our time on the way back, stopping to look in shop windows and that. I really like my new jacket and hat and scarf, and when we stop and chat with a couple of people from the house, they say how smart I look. I try and catch my reflection in the shop windows we go past, just to see what me and Marie look like together. I reckon we look pretty good.

We're walking past this telly shop when Marie suddenly stops and goes back a couple of steps.

'We're on TV,' she says, pointing into the window.

There's loads of TV sets in the window and I dunno which one to look at.

'This one – here.' She waves with one hand and points with another. There's a small black and white set, and I can see two people on it, with one of them waving a hand.

'Is it us?'

'Look,' she says, pointing at a camera in the window. 'We're being filmed. Wave your hand and watch the screen.'

I do like she says. It's really weird seeing yourself on telly. It ain't like looking in a mirror cos I ain't looking straight at myself, but sort of down from above.

'I always fancied being on TV,' Marie says, giving a bow. 'Marie, Queen of Scots – prima ballerina.'

She starts humming and doing these dance steps. I move to one side so it's just Marie on the telly, and watch her. It's like watching a proper programme. It ain't really like ballet, but it looks sort of real – you know, like Candid Camera or summat. She finishes her dance and I clap. Then she grabs my hat and sticks it on her head.

'I say, I say, I say,' she says in this funny voice.

She's going to tell a joke, and I start laughing already.

'Did you hear about the Irishman who took his car in for a service? He couldnae fit it through the church doors!'

She takes the hat off and does a couple of dance steps. I'm laughing like crazy now.

'What's yellow and dangerous?' she asks.

'I dunno!' I yell, looking at the telly screen.

'Shark infested custard! How do you fit four elephants into a Mini?'

'I dunno!'

'Two in the front and two in the back!'

She does a little dance, making a noise like a trombone, then she bows and the hat falls off.

I give her a clap and turn round. She's grinning at me, her eyes all sparkly.

'Your turn, Billy.'

She hands me the hat and moves me into the middle of the pavement.

'Ladies and gentlemen, boys and girls,' I start.

Marie's got her back to me, watching the telly.

'Mr Billy Bayswater will now sing you a song. The name of it is – "Old MacDonald had a farm".'

Marie gives a little cheer, and I clear my throat.

'Old MacDonald had a farm – ee-aye-ee-aye-oh.

And on that farm he had a – '

I can't think what animal to do.

'Duck,' Marie says.

'With a – '

'Quack, quack here,' she says.

'And a quack, quack there.'

'Here a quack.'

'There a quack.'

'Everywhere a quack, quack.'

We're falling about laughing. I'm trying to flap my arms like a duck and quack at the same time. These couple of kids are watching us like we're mad, but we just carry on.

'Old MacDonald had a farm – ee-aye-ee-aye-oh.'

We go through the whole song with both of us making the noises and me doing the actions. The funniest one was the horse. We was laughing so much we couldn't get no sound out. And when I pretended to be a horse I got so excited I bumped into this litter bin and fell over.

When we finish we're hanging onto each other. We've been laughing so much we're weak. Marie's eyes are all wet and she can't stop giggling. She tries to keep a straight face, but she keeps cracking up.

'Home we go, hen. I can't take any more of this.'

We take each other's hand and start walking. We don't say nothing on the way back, but sometimes we just burst out laughing for no reason at all.

Sometimes Marie gets letters. You know, from friends and that. When she gets one she usually reads it out to me. Marie used to live in Scotland and sometimes her friends write to her. I like it when Marie gets a letter, cos I never get one – except my giro cheque. I wish I had a friend who'd write to me. It must be nice to get letters and that.

One morning, Marie gets this letter and she sort of reads it quick. Just to herself – you know, not out loud like she normally does. I ask her if it's from Betty, her best friend in Scotland, but she says it ain't. She looks pretty shook up from the letter.

'Who's it from then, Marie?' I ask her.

She hesitates a bit, like she don't want to say. Then she stuffs the letter back in the envelope and chucks it on the side.

'From my husband,' she says.

For a minute I'm pretty confused. I never knew Marie had a husband. I thought she was single, like.

'We bust up a while back,' she says.

It's pretty sunny and there's a patch of white light on the floor by my foot. I sort of dabble my foot in it like it's a puddle. I never knew Marie was married. Maybe she told me and I forgot. The puddle suddenly disappears and I look over at Marie. She's frowning like she's thinking real hard.

'I never knew you was married,' I say.

She sighs and picks up the envelope again. 'It wasn't much of a marriage. We fought like hell for most of the time. That's why I left – he kept beating me up.'

I remember Marie's face when it was all bashed up. Maybe her husband did that.

'Does he live in Scotland?'

She nods and pulls the letter out again. I watch her face when she reads through it. It's hard to believe Marie's got a husband. I suppose she's old enough and that, but it's still hard to believe. I always thought she was single.

Even though she tries to hide it, I can see she's pretty upset by the letter. When she's finished reading it again I ask her what's the matter.

'Nothing,' she says a bit sharp like. 'He's finally getting out, so now I can move back.'

She looks at me for a bit, then she goes over to the drawer and takes out another envelope. This one's got some photos in it. She looks at them for a bit and then hands them over to me. They're pictures of a little girl. She's dressed in this furry pink thing, and she's got these little white shoes on. She looks real pretty with her yellow hair. In one of the pictures she's sitting on a lady's knee. At first, cos I'm looking at the baby, I don't see who the lady is. Then I have a closer look and see that it's Marie. She looks a bit different to now. Her hair's shorter in the picture and she's a bit fatter.

Marie comes behind me and looks over my shoulder. 'That's Josephine. She'll be two in February.'

I don't really hear Marie cos I'm thinking. It's funny, but I sort of recognise the baby. She reminds me of someone I seen – someone I knew really well. I think about it real hard, but I can't remember who it is.

It's a bit annoying like, cos I can't remember, so I give Marie back the pictures.

'She's in care,' she says, looking at the photos again. 'If I can move back to my place, they'll let me have her back.'

'Who is she?' I ask. Maybe I've met her with Marie before and that's why I recognise her.

'She's my daughter, Billy.'

I stare at Marie. I don't understand.

She slides the photos into the envelope and then shoves them back in the drawer. 'I should've told you before.'

I shut my eyes real tight to try and stop the room going round. Marie's got a baby. She's got a husband and a baby and I never knew.

I open my eyes and look down at Marie's tummy. She would've been all fat there once, and a baby growing inside of her. Inside of Marie. I dunno if I'm happy or sad. Marie's got a baby.

I have to sit down cos I feel all dizzy. Marie pulls her boots on and says she's going out to get some fags. She looks a bit worried. She don't ask me if I want to go with her, but even if she did I wouldn't go. I got to think about this on my own. She sort of ruffles my hair and goes out.

After a minute I get up and go into my old room. There's still a couple of beat up chairs there and I sit down in one of them. I got to think about this.

I think real hard, but it's difficult to concentrate. Marie's got a husband and a baby. A husband and a baby. I look over at the posters on the wall. I ain't took them down cos Marie's got plenty of pictures on her walls. I look at each of them. They look pretty stupid now. There's that one of the man and the woman in the boat smiling at each other. I suppose they're married – I never thought about it before. I get up and look at the picture real close to see if there's a baby in the boat, but I can't see one.

Suddenly I start ripping the poster off the wall, ripping it into bits. I chuck them on the floor and kick at them. Bloody, bloody, bloody. I thought she was my girlfriend. I thought she liked me.

When I done that I feel a bit sorry. That was my favourite picture and now it's all ripped up. I'm crying a bit as I try and stick the pieces together, but I can't do it so I just leave them on the floor and sit back in the chair. I'm sorry I done that – it was a nice picture.

Life's confusing sometimes, you know. Like when you think you just got things figured out, they change all of a sudden. I thought Marie was my girlfriend. I didn't really want to marry her or nothing, but I thought, you know, that we was friends like. You know, like boyfriend and girlfriend. But now she's all married and stuff.

I stop my crying and just sit there a bit. I know people think I'm stupid, and I know they laugh at me and that. Most times I don't mind, but sometimes things get pretty confusing. Like this morning. You know, one minute I'm thinking Marie's my girlfriend, and then all of a sudden she says she's got a husband and that. Things'd be much easier if people didn't make it so complicated. It's people really, that make things difficult. I wish people would tell the truth.

Marie comes back in after a bit. I rub my face quick so she don't see I've been crying. She looks at the bits of paper on the floor, but she don't say nothing. I wish I'd hidden the bits – I feel silly ripping it up for nothing.

She squats down in front of me and puts her elbows on my knees. I turn away so I can't look at her, but she leans over and looks me straight in the face.

'What's up, Billy?'

Her nose is all cold and wet and I want to wipe it for her, but I don't. I would've yesterday, but things are different today.

'Come on, Billy. Tell me.'

She gives me a little smile and I feel a bit better.

'Are you still my friend?' I say, quiet like.

Her smile gets bigger, but she looks sort of sad. 'Of course I am.'

I'm still not sure if she means it or not. 'But you got a husband.'

'I *had* a husband. Not any more.' She rubs the tops of my legs like I'm cold and she's trying to warm me up. 'Won't you forgive me for keeping it a secret?'

A door slams along the corridor and I can hear music coming from upstairs. Suddenly everything's OK. I'm at home and Marie's with me, and she's still my friend.

'I really like you, Marie,' I say. Suddenly I get all laughy, cos Marie's my friend and I'm happy.

'And I really like you too, hen.'

81

She pats my knee and stands up. 'Are you coming to the house meeting? Remember? You said you would.'

I look up at her. She's standing with her back to the window and I can see a sort of thin blue light round her body. She looks real pretty standing there with her old coat on. I jump to my feet and give her a hug, and she pats my back.

'Easy does it, Billy. Don't get too excited.'

The meeting's in the big room upstairs. It's where the bands practise. I can't remember what band Petra's in, but I seen them practise once. They were OK, but I didn't think they was brilliant.

There's old mattresses up against all the walls and someone's stuck hundreds of egg boxes on the ceiling. Marie says it's to keep the noise in, but I don't reckon it works too well, cos you can hear them all over the house when they practise. It was pretty interesting watching Petra's band practise. They don't know any songs all the way through, and they kept stopping. Petra sings with them. She tries real hard, but she don't really sing – she sort of shouts.

There's about ten people when we come in, sitting on the floor. I don't know all the people in the house yet – there's too many, and new people are always coming. I sit down on the floor next to Marie and look round. One of the window's been smashed and someone's stuck newspaper over the hole. Dirty Dave's decorated most of the walls and mattresses. He's pretty young – only about my age, and he paints a lot of the walls in the house – you know, with felt pens and spray cans and that. I don't really like his drawings – it's mostly words and rude pictures. To tell the truth, I find it pretty embarrassing, but nobody seems to mind. He wanted to do Marie's room, but she wouldn't let him.

We sit around for a bit, chatting. Daggy comes over and talks with me and Marie a bit. She's OK, is Daggy – she's a friend of Sonja's. She's an artist, but I ain't seen none of her paintings. I spect she's better than Dirty Dave.

Suddenly someone bangs on the drum in the corner, and we all look up. It's Peter.

'OK everybody. Listen up.' He does a little drum roll and hits a cymbal. I give a little laugh and Peter looks over at me and hits it again, harder this time. I like Peter – he's a good laugh.

'I hereby call this meeting to order.'

Everyone claps a little and Peter sits down on the drum stool. He twirls the stick in his hand and crosses his legs.

'And the agenda, members of the board is . . . shit.'

Someone gives a little cheer, and Peter holds up his hand. 'Not just any shit, but the turds laid by – ' He twirls the stick again and then points at someone I never seen before. 'Coprophile Colin.'

There's another lot of clapping. I join in, even though I ain't sure what's going on.

'As anyone who graces the top floor knows, Colin is turning his room into a cess pit. The bog, dear members of the board, *may* be a bourgeois invention, and perhaps Colin's biodegradable crap is a true anarchist statement, but some of you are finding the stink of revolution too much.'

'Hold on, Peter,' Colin says all of a sudden. He's got a brown beard and he looks pretty ill. Sort of dirty. 'Macrobiotic shit doesn't smell!'

'But why don't you use the goddam bog?' someone says.

They all look at Colin, waiting for him to answer. He's confused for a bit.

'But what's wrong with crapping on newspaper and emptying it out every now and then? It doesn't stink.'

'Bullshit man!' A black boy shouts. 'I have to live next to you and it stinks like fuck!' He shouts this pretty loud. I don't like it when people shout. It scares me a bit to tell the truth. It gets pretty confusing after this. Everyone starts talking at once – some of them shouting and others just laughing. Colin's getting pretty flustered and red in the face. Marie don't say nothing and nor does Peter. I look over at him while everyone's arguing and he smiles and winks at me like he's really enjoying himself. I don't really know what's going on, but everyone's arguing about summat.

They carry on arguing for a bit, then Peter hits the cymbal again. Everyone shuts up.

'Let's find out what Billy thinks about this,' Peter says. Someone laughs, but I can see from Peter's face that he ain't making a joke.

I dunno what to say and I look down at my feet. To tell the truth, I wasn't really listening to what everyone was saying.

'Should Colin use the bog like everyone else?' Peter says.

I think about it for a bit. Satan don't use the toilet neither. He goes on a newspaper in Marie's room. It stinks a bit, but I reckon it's OK for a cat to do that, cos a cat's an animal. But I dunno why Colin don't use the toilet. It's all pretty confusing cos Colin ain't a cat or nothing, so why don't he use the toilet? I don't really know what to say, so I just look at Marie. Everyone's quiet, waiting for me to say summat. Marie nods at me and smiles. I wish Peter wouldn't ask me difficult questions. I don't like talking about toilets and stuff – it's dirty.

'Why are you so interested in – ' I stop and go red a bit.

'In what, Billy?'

'In . . . dirty.'

Everyone laughs and I think I said the wrong thing, but Peter smiles at me and stands up.

'Meeting over,' he calls out. 'The zen patriarch has spoken.'

After the meeting, me and Marie go to Peter's room. I been there before. I really like it – it's got these carpets over the walls and lots of interesting stuff like a museum or summat. It's real cosy, specially if he's got the fire on.

He's got loads of interesting things like wooden masks

84

and a big metal pipe for smoking and a little brass bell. He lets me look at them when I come to see him. He's nice like that, is Peter – you know, he don't wait for me to ask – he just says 'Make yourself at home, Billy' or 'Have a look at this,' or 'Guess where I got this?'

My favourite is his glass ball. It's like a big marble – real heavy, like – and when you look through it everything goes upside down. I like looking through it. It's a bit like at the swimming baths when you open your eyes under water. If you hold it in your hands it gets warm. I like that bit of it.

I get on and look through Peter's stuff while Marie talks to him. I don't pay them too much attention cos I'm busy, but I think Marie shows him the letter she got this morning.

Peter's got this long arrow in his room. It's wood with a teeny metal bit at the end and red feathers. He told me the story about where he got it – it was real interesting, and a true story – not a made-up one. I've forgot the story, but it was real interesting. I ask him if he'll tell me the story again, but he just looks over at me and shakes his head. They're looking pretty serious, Marie and Peter. I spect it's summat to do with the letter. I try and remember what the letter was about, but I've forgot. Summat about her husband. And a baby.

I don't like it when grown-ups get all serious and that. Often bad things happen after – you know, like you're taken away to school, or they tell you someone died or summat like that. I sort of get that feeling now – you know, like summat bad's going to happen.

'Come and sit down here, Billy,' Peter says, patting the sofa he's sitting on. I got the glass ball in one hand and the arrow in the other. I can't remember where they go, but Peter tells me to bring them too, so I go and sit on the sofa next to him.

When I get older I'm going to have gold teeth like Peter – I reckon they look real good.

I roll the glass ball round in my hand a bit, waiting for them to say summat. It looks like they're going to say summat bad on account of how serious they're looking. Sometimes I wish bad things wouldn't happen.

'Where's your family, Billy? Your mum and dad?' Peter asks all of a sudden.

I carry on rolling the ball. I can see colours inside of it.

He asks the question again, but I don't say nothing. The glass ball's pretty warm now and I press it to my cheek and sort of roll it against my skin.

'Have you got any family, Billy? Can you remember them?'

I start hitting the arrow on the side of my leg, making this whacking sound like Mrs Seaton beating the rugs on the washing line. Whack, whack, whack, she used to go and clouds of dust would fly all about. It used to make me and Annie sneeze if we got too close.

'Come on,' Marie says like she's playing a game. 'Won't you tell us?'

I go on whacking the side of my leg. Mrs Seaton's husband died so she didn't have no money – that's why she worked for us. I like Mrs Seaton. She's fat and she used to cuddle me and Annie. She smells nice too – like flowers and soap. And when she whacked the rugs me and Annie used to sneeze on account of the dust.

Peter takes the arrow away from me. 'You'll hurt yourself,' he says, slipping it under the sofa.

Marie and Peter are watching me with a sort of worried look on their face. I wonder if I'm going to have a fit, and that's why they're watching me. I hope I won't have a fit. I don't understand why they're talking about Mrs Seaton.

'I miss her, you know.'

'Who?'

'Mrs Seaton.'

It's getting pretty dark. I can hardly see the things on the table in the corner.

'Who's Mrs Seaton?' Peter asks.

That surprises me when he says that, cos I thought he

knew who Mrs Seaton was. 'She looks after me and Annie,' I tell him.

I want to get summat else to play with and I try and get up, but Peter holds me by the arm.

'Just a sec, Billy. Who's Annie?'

'I seen a photo of her,' I say. 'She's wearing this pink thing, and she's got these white shoes.'

I hear Marie go 'Ah', and Peter looks at her quick.

'Annie's your sister, isn't she. You told me about her once didn't you, Billy,' Marie says.

I nod.

'About how you used to play together.'

I shut my eyes and sort of squeeze my legs to my chest. I really like Annie. She's my best best friend.

'How old is she, Billy?'

I open my eyes and think about it for a bit. 'This high,' I say, holding my hand out. 'But she grows real quick.'

'So, when did you last see her?'

'Ages ago.'

I really miss Annie, now I think about her. We used to play together real well – that's what Mrs Seaton said. I used to help her with things – you know, things that little kids can't do too well, like cutting up their food and opening doors and stuff like that. And she used to make up these stories and tell them to me. Real good stories too, just like they was from a book. Annie was real clever – even though she was only a little kid, like. I wish I could see Annie again, but they took me away, and they wouldn't let me see her again.

'Where do Annie and Mrs Seaton live, Billy? Can you remember?'

I wish they'd stop asking all these questions – I'm getting a bit confused. And I wish they wouldn't ask about Mum and Dad and Annie and Mrs Seaton. It makes me all upset when I think about them.

I don't want them to ask me any more questions, so what I do is I lie back in the sofa and shut my eyes like I'm asleep. I feel real tired all of a sudden.

I can hear Marie and Peter talking soft, but I don't listen to them. I don't want to talk no more.

When I open my eyes again it's nearly dark. I can see two orange spots of light where Marie and Peter are smoking fags. They ain't talking no more.

Marie turns to look at me, and I can just see the light shining off her eyes. 'What about some crumpets for tea?' she says.

It's getting nearly Christmas now. I dunno how long we got to wait, but it's pretty soon. The shop round the corner's selling these Christmas trees. They ain't got no lights on or nothing like that, but they're real nice all the same. If you stick your hand in them it's all prickly cos they got these tiny little leaf things and they prick. The best thing about them is their smell. They smell real good, I reckon.

I want to buy a Christmas tree and decorate it like we used to at school but Marie says we ain't got enough money. That's a shame, that is, cos I really like Christmas trees. They're all Christmassy and that.

I bought some Christmas cards all on my own. I went into this shop and got a little box of them. I wasn't with Marie or nothing – I was all on my own, like. I was pretty pleased with myself. They're real nice cards – there's some that got pictures of a blue sky with a big white star and some men on a camel and that. And there's some of baby Jesus in his bed with all these cows and sheep and stuff looking at him all gentle like. Baby Jesus was real poor, so he had to grow up on a farm and that, and when he got bigger he went round with some friends telling everyone about God, and then he died. Mr Browne said Jesus died cos we're all bad, but I dunno about that. I reckon he died cos he wanted to go back to his home in Heaven and be with God. You see, it wasn't his real home here – his real home was up in Heaven with God and the angels. He was only visiting earth like, so he could tell people about God and that. I don't blame Jesus for wanting to go home.

Jesus was good though. I like him a lot. He went round

with some seeds, planting them in the ground and that, but some of them grew and some of them didn't. It's always that way – I dunno why, but it is. You can try real hard, but it don't make no difference – sometimes a plant won't grow no matter what you do.

Anyway, they're real nice cards. I wish I had someone to send them to.

The electric shop down the road's got these fairy lights in the window. You know, for Christmas, like. They leave them on all night, even when the shop's shut. It's real great to watch them cos they blink on and off all the time. They're all round the window. They don't half look pretty.

When I go out to the shops – you know, to get stuff like milk or fags for Marie or summat – I always stop a bit and watch them. I wish it was Christmas all the time. It's nice when people put fairy lights in shop windows and stuff. They should do it all the time I reckon.

Marie says there's a street in town that's all lit up with Christmas lights – you know, all across the street and that. She says she might take me to see them. I'd really like that, I would – I really like Christmassy things.

I dunno, but there's summat up with Marie. She's been a bit funny these last couple of days, like summat's bothering her or summat. I dunno what's up, but I reckon summat is.

And then I find out. We're walking back from the shops – me and Marie – and we stop for a bit to look at the lights in the electric shop. She's pretty patient, Marie is. I know she ain't really interested in shop windows and that, but she don't mind waiting while I have a look.

It's getting dark, so the lights look extra pretty, flashing on and off. It's pretty good cos when the lights go off I can see me and Marie in the window like it's a mirror – and then when the lights come on, we disappear. There's summat about these lights that remind me of Annie – I dunno what it is. Maybe we had some lights like it once. I reckon that's it, cos they look sort of familiar.

I'm watching the lights and that, and then suddenly Marie says summat.

'I've got to go away, Billy,' she says.

I don't want to turn round cos the lights are on at the moment.

'Where to?' I say, still looking at the window.

'Scotland. I'm moving back in with my baby.'

I keep forgetting Marie's got a baby. It's still pretty odd when I remember – you know, that Marie's a mum and that. The lights are off for a bit, so I turn round to look at her.

'Is Scotland a long way?'

'Yes. A long, long way.'

I've had enough of the lights, so we turn round and head back to the house. Raven passes by on the other side of the street, but he don't notice us.

'When are you coming back, Marie?'

'I won't be coming back.'

We carry on walking a bit. It's blummin freezing and the pavements are a bit slippy so we have to walk careful like.

'Will I go with you?' I ask.

She stops and looks at me. She looks pretty sad, like she's got some bad news. I reckon I know what's coming.

'I can't look after you any more, Billy.'

I scrunch up my face to stop myself from crying. I get this sort of aching feeling in my nose, and I give it a rub. I knew summat bad was coming. I knew Marie was going to say summat.

'Who'll look after me?' I ask after a bit.

'I'm going to get in touch with your social worker. What's his name?'

A cat nips across the pavement in front of us and slides through a gap in the fence. I try and see where it went, but it's too dark.

'Mr Jackson,' I say. I can't look at Marie. I'd cry if I

90

did, so I look down at my feet. I don't want to be looked after by Mr Jackson. I don't want Marie to go away.

The street lamps are on, making the pavements all fuzzy and silvery like fish. You got to be careful when the pavements are frosty cos you can slip and hurt yourself. Why isn't Marie going to stay here? – it's OK here. She's got Satan and a nice room and her record player and all that. Why's she got to go away?

It ain't far back to the house, but it takes ages cos we got to walk slow. I got this sort of tight feeling in my throat all the way back – you know, like I'm going to cry. I don't want to cry, and I sort of hold myself in when we walk back, but I don't half feel sad. We don't say nothing – we just walk.

When we get back to the house, Marie gives me the key to the door and I unlock it and let her go in first. There's someone's motorbike in the hall, and we got to squeeze past it.

I been trying to think all the way back, but I can't figure it out. It's all so sudden like, Marie going away and that.

She switches the light on in her room, and I go in and sit straight down on the chair. I don't take off my coat or nothing – I just sit down. I feel really miserable to tell the truth. I was OK till Marie told me she was going away, and now I feel all sad. Marie looks at me like she's waiting for me to say something.

'I don't want Mr Jackson to look after me. I want you to.'

Marie squints like she's hurt herself and squats down by the chair. She's still got her hat on, and her hair is all tucked up inside. 'Can't you understand, Billy? I've got my own life to lead.'

I start crying now. I try not to, but I just can't stop.

'I don't want you to go.'

Marie leans forward and sort of hugs me. I'm crying like mad now – I just can't stop. Marie strokes the back of my head, but it just makes it worse.

I don't understand why she's got to go. Everything's great here. She's my friend. She can't go and leave me.

Why do people always leave you? As soon as you get to really like someone, they go off and leave you. Like Sara at school who died. Sometimes I think God is pretty cruel. All I want is some friends, but as soon as I get some real good friends they go off and leave me. It ain't fair I reckon. It just ain't fair.

On Marie's last night, we had a sort of party in her room. Marie's got loads of friends, and they all came to say goodbye. We had a pretty good time I suppose, but to tell the truth I didn't feel like a party much.

I'm going to miss Marie. She's my best friend.

Marie left this morning. I gave her a hand packing up her clothes and stuff. She's only got two suitcases, so she had to leave a lot of stuff behind – like her tailor's dummy and all the furniture. She sold her record player to Eric from the top floor. She said I could keep any of the stuff she left behind, or sell it if I wanted, but I dunno about that. She couldn't take Satan with her, so she asked me to look after him. She told me how much food to give him every day, and to be sure to leave the window open a bit so he could get into the garden and do his business. I don't mind looking after Satan – it's a bit of company.

Marie took a taxi to the station on account of her bags being so heavy. I wanted to go with her to the train, but she told me to stay at home otherwise I'd get lost on the way back. It was real sad saying goodbye to Marie. I think she was sad too, cos her eyes watered like she was going to cry. I really didn't want her to go, but she had to. I helped her put her bags into the taxi and then we sort of kissed goodbye. I was brave and didn't cry or nothing, but I was real sorry to see her go. She was the best friend I ever had.

Marie said I could stay in her room, and she left a lot of stuff so it'd be comfy, but to tell the truth I feel real sad in there on my own. It looks all lonely like with Marie's bits and pieces gone. She took the material off of the wall, and all her shoes and make up and just about everything 'cept the big stuff. She said I could stay in her room, but I ain't going to. Marie's gone and left me. I dunno why, but she did – just like Annie and Sara. And now it's just me. All on my own. I wish Marie was still here.

I want to sleep in my old room, so what I do is take the mattress and stick it back in my old room. Marie's left me her sleeping bag and all the blankets so I'm OK for sleeping and that. She also left her electric fire, so I take that in too. I stick the fire on in my room and warm myself by it for a bit. It's flipping cold today, so I'm real glad I got an electric fire. I got to be careful about remembering to switch it off. It's dangerous if you leave it on all night – you can start a fire and that if you ain't careful.

It ain't too bad – you know, with the sleeping bag and the electric fire and that, but I still feel miserable. If Marie was here then I'd be OK, but she ain't. She's gone to Scotland to look after her baby. She's got a little girl, Marie has. I know cos she showed me a picture once. I wish she didn't have to go.

I dunno what to do. Normally, Marie and me'd get a cup of coffee and then sit by the fire and chat. She'd have a fag with her coffee, and I'd sit and watch the smoke making patterns in the air, and it'd be quiet and it'd be just her and me.

I go back into her room and have a look around. It's funny in here with everything all different. Marie's gone to Scotland to look after her baby, so everything's going to be all different and Mr Jackson's going to look after me.

I think about making some coffee, but I don't bother in the end – it ain't worth it just for me. Marie's left most of her pictures on the wall, and I have a look at them. She was always cutting pictures out of magazines and sticking them on her wall. There's a photo of a cat sitting on a chair, licking its paws. I stuck that one on the wall. I liked that picture so Marie let me cut it out and stick it on the wall. I try to take it off so I can keep it, but the paper tears. I stick the bits in my pocket anyway. It's a nice picture – it'd be a shame to just chuck it away. Marie's left a load of mags behind, so I pick one up and have a flick through it. When I open it, a load of bits of paper fall out and flutter to the ground. I don't bother to pick them up. No one lives here no more, so it don't matter.

I try and stop myself, but I just start crying. I know it ain't grown up and that but I can't stop myself. I feel so sad with Marie gone. I wish she hadn't gone away.

I go back to my room and lie on the bed. I end up staying there for ages, thinking about Marie and that. She said she'll send me a letter, but I reckon it's too early to go and have a look. I'll ask Sonja tomorrow to see if there's a letter for me. It's nice that she's going to send me a letter. That makes me feel a bit better, but I still dunno when I'm going to see her again. She's a long way away.

I didn't get up all day till it got dark and Mr Jackson came. He wasn't very pleased with me, and told me off for not saying where I'd moved to. He said I can't go on living here, not on my own like. He's going to try and get me into Combe Court. I don't want to go to Combe Court. It smells.

Mr Jackson stayed quite a bit. He wanted to know how I'd been getting on, and who'd been helping me out. I told him all about Marie and showed him the pictures we took in that photo booth. He wasn't very interested in Marie. He just sort of glanced at the photos and then carried on talking. Mr Jackson's always busy.

He told me he'd come back tomorrow, and then he went off. He asked me if I'd had anything to eat today. I said yes, cos I thought I had, but to tell the truth, I ain't sure now. I don't want to see Mr Jackson tomorrow, but I didn't tell him that. I try to like Mr Jackson, but to tell the truth, he ain't all that friendly. He pretends to be, but he ain't really I reckon.

When Mr Jackson went I just carried on lying there. It

got dark pretty soon after, but I didn't bother to move. I just stayed there listening to people moving around upstairs.

I spend a long time thinking about Marie and some of the things we done together. Like swimming and shopping and that. I wish Marie was here so we could talk about it.

When I wake up, I know summat's up when I open my eyes and see it's all bright, but it takes me a minute to remember where I am. Marie's room's sort of dark in the morning on account of the curtains, but my room ain't got no curtains so it's real bright. When I see I'm in my old room, I remember Marie's gone. I was OK when I woke up, but when I remember Marie's gone I start feeling sad.

It's extra cold today and I don't want to get up. Normally I'd get up and make me and Marie a cup of coffee, but there ain't no point now, so I stay in bed.

I got a bit of a headache on account of how cold it is and I snuggle back into my sleeping bag. I listen for noises, but it's real quiet. I think everyone's asleep except for me – I can't hear nothing apart from the traffic.

I don't want to get up. Normally I would, to make the coffee and that, but there don't seem no point now. Marie's gone so I ain't got no one to make coffee for. I wish she was here and everything was OK again.

I dunno what to do. I try to go to sleep again, but I ain't sleepy, and I get all fidgety. I might as well get up – I could do with summat to eat, to tell the truth.

It's really flipping cold today, so I get dressed as quick as I can. I switch on the fire and warm my hands for a bit. I got to remember to be careful with the fire. Marie told me to be sure to switch it off when I ain't in the room, or else at night when I'm sleeping.

I really don't want to go to Combe Court. I want to stay here with Marie and Satan and Peter and the rest of them. It ain't fair.

Once I'm a bit warmer, I go into Marie's room and have a look for the cornflakes. Marie left some food for me – some coffee and cereal and a bit of bread. Normally we'd buy our meals from the downstairs kitchen, but for breakfast we had our own food so we didn't have to get up till late. Anyhow, Sonja and Petra never did breakfast. I always enjoyed that, having breakfast in bed.

Satan's miaowing, so I feed him first. I think I forgot to feed him yesterday, I can't remember. I got to be more grown up if I'm going to look after a pet.

Marie bought loads of cat food before she left, so there's plenty for him. I fill up his new dish to the top and stick it on the floor. He's real excited when I'm shoving the food into his dish – rubbing against my legs and miaowing like crazy. I suppose he must be real hungry if I didn't feed him yesterday. He gulps down the food real quick, spilling bits onto the floor. I wonder if Satan misses Marie. I don't suppose so – all Satan's interested in is food.

I get the milk carton from the window and pour it over my cornflakes. At first when I tip it up nothing comes out, then it all sort of glugs into the bowl. I shake it a bit and hear a rattling, so I look inside. There's a lump of ice floating in the carton. I try and get it out with my fingers, but I can't reach it so I pour it into another bowl and put it on the floor for Satan to drink. It must be pretty cold for the milk to freeze, I reckon. It wasn't even in a fridge or nothing – it was just pressed up against the window to keep it cold.

I sit down in the armchair and eat my cereal. The milk's so cold it makes my teeth ache. Normally I like breakfast, but the milk's too cold and it's making my face ache. I want to leave it, but I carry on till I'm finished. You got to eat all your food up cos there's children in the world who's starving.

Satan won't touch the milk – it must be too cold for him too. When he's finished eating, he starts washing himself. I really like that about cats – the way they keep themselves clean. He finishes after a bit and then jumps up on the window ledge. The window's shut and he turns round and looks at me.

'You want to go out, Satan boy?' I say.

He don't understand me of course, but he miaows like he's saying yes. I'm glad I got Satan – it's someone to talk to. We weren't allowed to keep pets at school. Mr Browne had a gerbil in a cage in the classroom, but we weren't allowed to take it to the dorms – it had to stay in the classroom. That's one reason I don't want Mr Jackson to send me to Combe Court – they wouldn't let me keep Satan.

I get up and open the window, then I see Satan's done a job on the floor by the chair. Marie would be mad if she saw that, so I rip a page from one of her mags and scrape it up.

'Naughty Satan,' I say, looking cross at him. 'You shouldn't've done that.'

It's my fault really, cos the window should've been open. I got to remember things like that.

I let Satan out and chuck the paper in a drawer. If Mr Jackson sees me all grown up, then maybe he'll let me stay here.

I rinse the bowl in the sink. The water's real cold, but I wash my face anyhow. I got to look after myself. I got a toothbrush somewhere but I can't find it now everything's changed. It used to be in the blue mug, but Marie took that. I don't spect she's took my toothbrush – she probably put it somewhere. I look round the room, but I can't find it. So, what I do is, I just sort of rub my teeth with my fingers. I use toothpaste and that, so I suppose it works OK.

Then I remember it's the next day and there'll be a letter from Marie. For a second I get so excited, I have to calm myself down. I'd forgot! I rush out into the hall, down to the front door. The postman's been – there's some letters on the side. I pick them up and look at the envelopes. I look for one starting with a 'B' cos I know what that looks like. It takes me quite a while to go through them cos I check every one careful like. A couple of them's got 'B's in them and I try and work out which one's for me, but it's too hard. Some of them are typed and some are written – you know, by hand like. I dunno if Marie's got

97

a typewriter – she never told me. I feel each letter to see if I can guess which one's mine. There's a fat one. I hope it's that one. I hope it's a good long letter. And maybe photos too – that'd be great.

I get a bit flustered with all the letters, so what I do is, I take them all and go to Sonja's room. I bang on the door, but no one answers, so I push it open and go in. Sonja's still in bed asleep. I tiptoe over to her bed and give her a nudge. I have to shake her quite hard before she wakes up.

Sonja looks real different without all her make up. She looks sort of young looking. She grumbles a bit about me waking her up, but I don't think she minds all that much. She's pretty kind. I give her the letters and ask her which one's for me, and she looks through them quick.

'There is no letter for you, Billy,' she says, handing them back and shutting her eyes. I think she's pulling my leg, so I ask her again.

'There's nothing,' she says.

I want her to check through them again. She must've made a mistake – Marie said she'd write to me. Sonja sighs and looks through them again.

'She only went yesterday, Billy. It's too early for a letter.'

She shuts her eyes again and rolls over. I look at the back of her head for a minute. Marie said she'd write to me. She said so. I want to ask Sonja if she thinks the postman lost it, but I stop myself. I'll ask her later.

I go back downstairs and put the letters back. I'm real disappointed about that. I don't understand. Marie said she'd write to me. Summat must've happened.

I go back into Marie's room. I feel better with some of her stuff around me. I'm real disappointed about the letter. I can't figure it out, why she didn't write to me.

Marie's left her hairbrush. I don't think she meant to – I spect she forgot, cos it's a good brush and she used to use it all the time. I pick it up and brush it over my hand. I'm glad she forgot her hairbrush – it really reminds me of her. It's like she's still here – you know, having her hairbrush and that. There's some of her hairs in it, all long and black. I take a couple out and wind them round my finger. I really liked Marie's hair – it was real beautiful. I pretend Marie's in front of me and I'm brushing her hair like I used to.

'Well, Marie,' I say, pretending that she's sat there listening to me. 'What are we going to do today?'

I carry on brushing and act like she's talking back to me. We'll go to the park to see Mr Frost, she says. I nod and smile and just carry on brushing. She's sitting down with her back to me, just like she always used to, and I'm brushing slow and gentle, making her hair nice and neat. Then I do summat I ain't never done before. I put the brush on the side and carry on smoothing her hair with just my hands. I stop a bit and hold her head in my hands. Then I imagine she turns round and I lean over and kiss her on the mouth. I shut my eyes and hold my face to hers for a long time. I can smell Marie – the way her hair used to smell. We kiss for a long time, then I straighten up.

'Marie,' I say, looking down at her. 'Will you marry me?'

'Of course, Billy darling,' she says.

Then we're walking round the room and she's holding my arm like we're married and that. I've got this smart suit on and Marie's wearing this white wedding dress with all these frilly bits. All these people are watching us and clapping like mad cos they're so happy and proud of us. I walk round the room sort of smiling and sometimes waving or stopping to talk to someone. I meet Mr Browne and introduce Marie.

'This is my wife, Mr Browne,' I say, all proud like.

Mr Browne says 'Pleased to meet you' and shakes Marie's hand. I can see Mr Browne is impressed cos I'm all married and my wife's so beautiful and I'm so grown up and that.

There's a loud bang on the front door and I jump. Mr

Jackson said he'd come today. I listen for a bit to hear if anyone's going to answer the door. I hope it ain't Mr Jackson.

I look round the room quick to make sure it's neat looking. I should've tidied up a bit – that would've made Mr Jackson think I'm grown up enough to look after myself, but it's too late now.

I go back to my room. My sleeping bag's on the floor, and I shove it on the bed quick. Then I see the electric fire's still on. I run over and switch it off. Marie told me I shouldn't leave it on when I ain't in the room, and here I am – the first day she's gone and I've gone and left it on. I'm so stupid. Why do I always forget things? I'll never be grown up if I keep forgetting things. Maybe Mr Jackson's right – I can't stay here on my own.

I start crying. I try real hard to be sensible and do things right, but they never work out. I dunno why, but they never do. It's not that I don't try – I *do*. It's just sometimes I can't manage. You know, I forget things and stuff like that. I'll never be married and grown up and all that stuff.

I miss Marie. I miss her more than I ever missed anyone. If she was here everything would be OK and Mr Jackson wouldn't want to take me away.

'What's the problem, Billy?'

I look up. Mr Jackson's standing in the doorway. I wipe my face on my sleeve. I wish Mr Jackson hadn't seen me crying – he'll think I'm a real baby.

'Nothing, sir.'

He comes over and sort of squeezes my shoulder. 'Don't you worry,' he says, 'I've got you a place in Combe Court. We'll just get your things together, then we'll be off.'

He looks at me, worried like. I've started crying again. I try to stop, but I just can't. I don't want to go to Combe Court.

'We'll drive there,' he says. 'You'd like that now, wouldn't you.'

I nod my head and a tear falls onto my hand. Mr Jackson drives me in his car sometimes for a special treat.

But now I don't want to go nowhere. I want to stay here.

Mr Jackson helps me get all my stuff together. I ain't really got much – just my clothes and that, so it don't take long. We stick all my stuff in the suitcase and sort of squash it down so it all fits in. I dunno what to do with the posters on the wall, and in the end I just leave them there. Maybe someone else would like to use them. I ask Mr Jackson if I can take all my plants, and he looks at them doubtful like.

'I don't know, Billy. There's an awful lot of them.'

He hums and haws for a bit then he says he'll put them in his car and ask if I can keep them at Combe Court. I hope so – I really like my plants.

Mr Jackson tells me to shove my dirty clothes in a placky bag, so I do that. The jigsaw won't fit in the suitcase. It's back in its box now, but it's still pretty big – so I have to stick it in with the dirty washing. I hope all the bits don't fall out of the box.

'Is this yours?' he says, holding up my new hat that Marie bought me.

'Yes, sir.'

He sticks it on his head and gives a big grin, like he's trying to cheer me up. I hold out my hand for the hat and he gives it to me. I dunno what to do with it, so I stick it on my head.

'Let's check the other room now, shall we?'

I follow him into Marie's room. I don't really like Mr Jackson being in here – I dunno why, but it's sort of private – you know, just me and Marie's like. Satan's back in and I suddenly remember I got to look after him. I tell Mr Jackson that, but he says I can't take him with me cos they don't let us keep pets at Combe Court. I dunno what to do about that. Marie asked me to look after Satan, and I suppose that makes him mine now. Mr Jackson says that maybe someone in the house can look after him. I think about that for a bit. I don't want no one else to look after him – *I* want to. It ain't fair, them not letting you keep pets in

Combe Court. I'm grown up enough to look after Satan. I know what to do and that – you know, how to feed him and how to leave the window open. It ain't fair I reckon.

I decide to go up and see Peter and ask if he'll look after Satan. I grab him and go upstairs. Peter ain't in, but his door's open, so I stick Satan on his bed and then shut the door quick so he won't try and run out. I reckon Peter'll look after him OK.

When I come back Mr Jackson is trying to shut my suitcase. It's pretty full and it won't shut proper. One of the clips is bust.

'Have you got any string we can tie this up with, Billy?' Mr Jackson asks.

I dunno, so I have a look round, but I can't find none. The shop on the corner sells string – I know cos I seen it – so I ask if I should go and buy some.

'Good idea,' he says. 'You go off and do that and I'll start loading your plants.'

I stick on my coat and jam the hat on so it won't come off in the wind. I ask Mr Jackson if he wants anything from the shop – you know, like fags or a newspaper or summat, but he says he don't. He checks I got enough money to buy the string, and then I go off.

When I'm walking to the shop I think a bit about moving and that. I hate moving to tell the truth. It's sort of sad leaving things behind. I don't understand why I always got to move. As soon as I get settled in some place, it's time to move on. And then you get put in a new place and you got to start all over again, finding where things are and making friends and that. I was real happy living here with Marie. I was getting real grown up and that – you know, looking after Satan and doing the shopping and that. Now I got to move and start all over.

I was right about the shop selling string, and I buy a nice ball of it – all clean and white. It looks pretty strong stuff – useful like.

I dunno. I just don't want to go back to Combe Court. I don't want to see Mr Jackson again neither. I really don't.

I hang around the pavement by the shop for a bit, fiddling with the ball of string in my pocket. It's flipping cold. I wish I had my woolly hat on, not my straw one. It's nearly Christmas I reckon. I reckon it's going to snow soon. It always snows at Christmas.

I dunno, but I just don't want to budge. I feel like staying outside the shop all day just watching the people go past and fiddling with this string in my pocket. It ain't fair, Mr Jackson making me go to Combe Court when I don't want to. I want to stay here.

Then I start walking. I know I'm going the wrong way, but I don't care. I ain't going back. I ain't never going to see Mr Jackson again.

I know my way round here and I know I'm going the wrong way, but I just carry on. I'll go back tonight and then I'll do summat. I'll run away or summat, or hide from Mr Jackson. I could go to Scotland to see Marie. She's still my friend – she'd like to see me, I bet.

I walk as quick as I can so Mr Jackson won't find me. I'll walk all day and then come back tonight. Peter'll help me – he's good at ideas. Maybe I can live at the house and hide if Mr Jackson comes round.

Anyway, I can't live at Combe Court. Marie said she'll write to me and she don't know where Combe Court is. And if she comes back to the house, she won't be able to find me, so I got to stay there.

And then I get a pretty good idea. Marie can come back to the house and bring her baby and we can carry on like before with me sleeping on the floor and that. I wouldn't mind that, even with the baby. Marie could look after the baby and I could help out by going to the shops for fags and milk and stuff like that. And then maybe Marie and me could even get married and I could sleep in her bed, and we could be all married and that. I should've said that to Marie – I reckon that would've been OK. Maybe when I go back tonight Sonja can write to Marie telling her that. I reckon it ain't a bad idea.

I get to this big main road with a park on the other side,

so I cross over careful and go in. I think I been here with Marie. I think it's where we watched the ducks once. I wish Marie was here now – she'd know what to do about Mr Jackson and Combe Court and that.

I wander round the park a bit looking at the trees and stuff. There ain't many people about – I suppose cos it's too cold.

There's still some old leaves that ain't been brushed up yet, so I kick at them as I go along. It's great, this park. It's nearly like being in the country. It'd be just like the country if there wasn't all the noise from the traffic. I been to the country once with Annie.

I try not to think about Mr Jackson and that. I feel a bit naughty to tell the truth, going off like that and leaving Mr Jackson waiting for me. But I really didn't want to go to Combe Court. I think I'd rather live in the park than go to the smelly old place.

I was there before – at Combe Court. It was after I left school. I didn't like it. It wasn't just young people like at school, it was all sorts. Grown ups and all sorts. There was this really old bloke – everyone called him 'Captain'. I suppose he was a captain of a ship or summat when he was younger. I didn't really like him. He was real old. And dirty too. He used to like me I think, but to tell the truth, I didn't like him much. He never shaved, and he used to smell real bad. He used to come and sit at my table when we had meals. I hated that, cos he used to eat all slobbery like – you know, dribbling and that. He was real old so I suppose he had trouble with his false teeth or summat, but anyway, it was pretty disgusting watching him eat. He tried to touch me once – you know, down there. That gave me a big shock that did, and after that I used to move away if he came too close to me. I don't like people doing things like that.

Captain'd been at Combe Court for ages and ages I think, cos he knew everyone, even the very poorly ones like Glenda. He knew all the nurses and doctors too. But even so I don't reckon he had any friends. Not real friends like. No one used to come and visit him. I reckon it was cos he was so dirty and ate so slobbery. I dunno, but I reckon that's real sad.

I can hear a woman calling 'Benjy, Benjy' and I turn round to see what's up. She's calling to a little dog which is running after summat with his tail wagging like mad. It's great to have a dog I reckon – they're more fun than cats. You can take dogs out for walks and teach them tricks and stuff. Me and Annie had a dog once I think. I ain't sure – I think it was us and not someone else. It was ages ago, so I've forgot. I think we had a dog, though. It had yellow hair and it used to swim in the sea when we chucked sticks for it. I think maybe it was called Simon – I ain't sure.

I carry on walking. It ain't like I'm going nowhere special – it's just so cold I got to move to keep from freezing. I think about the milk this morning, how it froze and it wasn't in a fridge or nothing. There's blood in your body, and I get to thinking about what would happen if your blood froze. You know, froze solid like a lump of ice. I reckon you'd be like one of them statues – all hard and cold, sort of stuck in one shape. I try it for a bit – you know, pretending that I'm all frozen, but someone on a bike comes down the path and I got to move to get out the way.

There's a wooden bench by the side of the path, so I sit down and stretch my legs out. My trainers are a bit wet from kicking the leaves but my socks are dry I think. I need a new pair of shoes, Marie said. My trainers are getting pretty worn out now. She said we'd get some in the sales, but I suppose it's too late now. She's in Scotland. I wish she wasn't. I wish she was here, sitting next to me on the bench, holding my hand like she used to.

It's pretty quiet apart from the traffic, and there's hardly anyone around. Sometimes people jog past, dressed up in tracksuits and that, but mostly I'm on my own.

I sit on that bench for quite a while – till it starts getting dark. Then suddenly I get all cold, and I have to jump around a bit to get warm. I wish I'd got my woolly hat. This straw one's real nice and that, but it ain't all that warm. I could do with a hot drink or summat – I'm froze.

I reckon I've waited long enough, and I can go back home now. I don't suppose Mr Jackson's waited all this time. I spect he's gone back to his office. I hope he ain't too angry at me. I didn't want to be naughty, but I really didn't want to go to Combe Court. But I spect he's gone now anyhow. What I can do is, I can go back and see if his car's still there. I know what his car's like – it's yellow, and he's got this sticker on the back window. I know cos he took me out in it sometimes. If it's gone, then I'll go back in and see Peter. Peter's clever – he'll have a good idea, I'm sure.

I start going back the way I came. I walk pretty quick to warm myself up. Just then, the street lights come on. It's funny, but when the lights come on, it suddenly seems more dark in the park. They look nice though, the lights – all warm and orangey. I'm looking forward to getting back home and sitting by the fire. I'll make a cup of coffee and toast some crumpets by the fire. Then I'll go and see Peter and see if he's got a good idea what I can do.

This park's blummin huge – I never knew it was so big. I carry on walking till it's really dark and all the cars have got their lights on. I got to cross the road – I remember that, so when I get to a gate I go out and have a look round. The road's real busy now – there's hundreds and hundreds of cars and buses all queuing up. It looks real nice with their headlights on and their little red lights at the back. Sort of Christmassy.

It's pretty difficult to cross the road on account of all the traffic, so I just carry on walking on the pavement. I don't feel too bad now – I'm pretty hungry, but I'm warm enough. Sometimes it's a bit like a dream, walking on my own down the pavement with all these car lights flashing in my face. It's OK like, but just a bit dizzy-making.

I carry on walking for quite a bit. There's more and more lights over the road – you know, from shops and that, and there's more people walking about. I ain't in any real hurry and I stop every now and then for a look round. I can't remember if I been here before or not – streets look all different at night from how they are in the day.

I got to cross the road, but I can't see no green man thing where I can cross safely. I got to be careful – cars just suddenly come out from nowhere and it's easy to have an accident. It's best if I don't go unless there's a proper green light thing. It's easy to have an accident, crossing the road.

There's an underground thing – you know, steps going down to a station, so I go down there and wander around for a bit. Some of the lights in the tunnel are busted, and it smells of piss. There's loads of rubbish around – cardboard boxes and paper and stuff, and there's this man under one of the lights, blowing into a mouth organ thing. He ain't playing a tune or nothing, he's just breathing in and out and making these weird noises, like rusty springs creaking or summat. There's a few people now and then going past, but no one stops.

I hang round by him, watching him for a bit. I dunno what he's doing. I think maybe he's blind, cos he's got his eyes shut. His cap's on the floor in front of him and I think about picking it up for him, cos maybe if he's blind he don't know he's dropped it. I leave it in the end – there's summat a bit scary about him. I run past him and up the steps to the street.

I'm pretty confused when I come out the other end. It's all different here – there's loads of shops and a cinema and that. I try and figure out if I crossed the road or not, but it's too confusing. I can't see the park no more, so it's hard to tell where I am.

There's this big roundabout with all these cars packed together and people on bikes slipping through the gaps in the traffic. It looks pretty nice with all the lights and buildings and that. There's this great big building thing like a bridge or a gate or summat with these spotlights on it. It looks real old and special, like summat in a museum or summat.

To tell the truth, I dunno where I am. I sort of recognise it, but I ain't sure – a lot of places look sort of the same. I have a think for a bit, then I start walking up the street I'm on. It looks pretty busy and there's loads of shops and that, so it might be the right way.

I don't mind this, walking along streets at night. I don't even mind being on my own. If I was with someone else I'd have to talk to them or hurry to keep up with them, but this way I can go at my own speed. I like looking in shop windows so I can take my time if I'm on my own. My favourite shops are ones with loads of lights in them, specially those coloured lights. There's quite a few restaurants with people in them having their tea. They look real nice restaurants – sort of posh. I'm pretty hungry by now but I don't go in. I never been to a restaurant – not on my own like. It's OK in a caff – you can just ask for egg and chips or if they have pictures you can just point, but I think I might have trouble in a restaurant cos you got to read from a menu thing, and I have a bit of trouble with my reading. I'd go in if Marie was with me, but I'm on my own and I might have a bit of difficulty with the menu. So instead, what I do is just stand outside and look through the window. There's this one with candles on the table in these little glass bowls, and it all looks cosy and nice. There ain't many people in there – I suppose cos it's too early for people to have their tea. There's a man and a woman sitting at a table by the window, and I watch them for a bit. They ain't eating yet, they're just drinking and talking. They don't see me, so they just carry on, real friendly and private like. It looks real nice, them sitting there, just the two of them. I wish Marie was here – we could go in and have a meal together.

I carry on up the street, looking in the windows. There's a TV shop with all these tellies on in the window, and I stop a bit and watch. I don't like telly all that much, but I stop anyhow. There's this person sitting on the pavement watching them. At first I think it's an old man, but then I see it's a lady. She's all wrapped up warm with this big old

108

coat on. She's got a trolley basket and a couple of placky bags full of stuff and she's made a sort of seat out of them so she's real comfy like. I dunno which telly she's watching cos there's three sets on, all with different programmes. She sort of glances at me and then she goes back to watching her programme. She looks real comfy there, like she's sitting in an armchair at home.

You can't hear nothing cos the glass is too thick, so you got to guess what the people are saying. I stay there a bit watching a telly programme with this man doing stuff. I think he's doing tricks and that, cos he's got hankies and playing cards and that. I don't really understand what he's doing, but it's OK to watch him for a bit.

The lady's watching a wildlife programme I reckon, cos all of a sudden she says 'I was bitten by a tiger once.'

I look over at her, but she don't say nothing else. She just carries on watching the telly. I dunno why she's talking about tigers cos there's horses on the telly. Maybe there was a picture of a tiger and I missed it.

She looks real comfy there and I think about sitting down for a bit and watching telly, but I ain't got nothing to sit on so I just carry on standing up. It's a pretty good idea I reckon – you know, if you ain't got a telly, to sit outside a telly shop. You can't hear the sound or nothing, but you can make that up.

After a bit I get bored and carry on walking up the street. I was going to say goodnight to the lady, but I stopped myself cos she looked so interested in the programme she was watching. I suppose she comes here every night with her bags and things cos she ain't got a telly at home.

I reckon I should nearly be home by now – I been walking for ages. I still dunno where I am, but I reckon I should be home pretty soon.

I go down this side street where there ain't so many big shops. There's shops and that, it's just they ain't so big and some of them ain't got lights on. I'm getting cold again, and my feet are aching with all this walking. I reckon I been walking for hours now.

I think about Mr Jackson and I get a sort of uncomfortable feeling when I remember he was waiting for me at the house and I didn't come back. I spect he was pretty angry about that. He was angry when I went off before and I didn't tell him I was living at the house with Marie. I feel in my pocket and find the ball of string I bought. I pull it out and have a look at it. It's pretty good stuff. It's real strong stuff. I'm glad I ain't at Combe Court now – that's where he was taking me to.

There's a sign for a railway station all lit up. There's caffs and that usually in railway stations. I could really do with a bit of a sit down and summat to drink, so I go down the driveway into the station.

It's blummin enormous inside – I didn't expect nothing like this. It's got this great high roof and loads of trains. It's real smoky and that. I like railway stations – you know, how big and noisy and busy they are.

I was right – there's a caff there, so I go in. It's like the dining room at school – all big and echoey. It's pretty nice though. It's got pictures on the walls and real flowers on the table. Usually flowers in caffs are plastic, but these ain't – they're really real. There's a young bloke cleaning the tables. He's wearing a paper hat – you know, like they do in caffs. A woman's washing the floor with a mop and a bucket. She looks like a nurse in her blue uniform and her scarf over her head. It's pretty quiet in the caff. There ain't no music playing or nothing like there usually is, just the sound of people talking and the clunking of the fruit machine.

I go up to the counter and have a look to see what they got to eat. It's pretty good here – they got photos of food all lit up over the counter so you can just point. I get real hungry looking at the photos – I ain't ate for ages. I feel in my pocket for my money and pull it out. My hands are real cold cos I lost my gloves and my fingers won't work proper – they're all sort of numb. I spread the coins out in my hand and have a look. It don't look like I got much – I ain't got no paper money. There's an old woman with thick glasses and a name tag who's serving the hot drinks so I go over to her and ask how much money I got.

She counts the money quick. '97p', she says.

'What can I get for that?' I ask her. I know it ain't much, but I dunno if it's enough to get a proper meal like.

She asks me what I want, and I think for a bit. 'Coffee,' I say. 'And that.' I point at the photo of a pie and chips. That looks pretty good – I dunno if it's steak and kidney or chicken, but either way would suit me fine.

'You haven't got enough for that, love,' she says, friendly like. 'If you really want coffee then all we've got are those buns or sweets.'

I think about it for a bit, then I ask her if I can afford some sandwiches.

'Not if you want a drink, love.'

I dunno what to do. I want a drink *and* summat to eat. In the end I decide to get a big cup of coffee and a jam doughnut.

I pay at the counter and get my change. Then I take my stuff over to the table by the window. My fingers are froze, so I warm my hands on the cup for a bit before I try drinking.

My hands are shaking so much I have to sip my coffee without picking it up – you know, by just sort of ducking my head and slurping it up. I know it ain't really polite, but my hands are shaking so much I'd spill it if I picked it up. After a bit I feel better so I start eating my doughnut. I chose the biggest one they had, and it's all glittery with sugar. The first bite I take makes all the jam squirt out the side over my chin. I ain't got a hankie or nothing so I try and lick it off with my tongue, but I can't get all of it. I can picture Marie – how she'd tell me off if she could see me. 'Oh, hen, you're a messy one,' she'd say with her laugh. She didn't really mind me making mistakes. She'd just laugh and say summat like that.

In the end I got to scrape the jam off with my finger. I try and eat the rest of the doughnut as neat as I can but I end up all sugary and sticky. I try wiping my fingers on my coat, but it don't help much – I still feel all sticky.

I still got a bit of coffee left after I finish eating the doughnut, so I sip it slow to make it last, and look round the caff.

There's three young kids – younger than me – playing at the fruit machine by the door. I dunno if they're friends or brothers. I reckon they're friends cos they don't really look like each other and there ain't no grown up with them, like they're a family out with their mum and dad. I watch them for a bit, but they don't win nothing. One of them's smoking a fag. I think he's trying to look all grown up and that, but he don't really – he just looks like a young kid trying to be grown up.

The bloke with the paper hat comes round with this trolley thing to clear the tables. He don't clear mine even though I'm finished, but when he goes past I ask if I can have a lend of his dishcloth to wipe my fingers. He don't mind me asking, and lets me use it. He goes off again when I give him his cloth back. He looks pretty bored.

There's a telephone on the wall just by my table and I think for a bit about who I'd like to phone. I got this real urge to speak to someone on the phone – I dunno who – just someone. I can't think of anyone I'd really like to speak to, except Marie of course, but I dunno if she's got a phone in Scotland. Even if she has, I ain't got her number. I wonder what it'd be like if the phone suddenly rung and it was for me. That'd be nice, that'd be – but I don't expect anybody would phone. That's a shame really, cos I'd like to talk to someone.

I sit there for a bit longer, till I finish my coffee, then I decide to go out and have a look round the station. I like railway stations with all their trains and whistles and that.

I dunno how tall it is, but the Christmas tree outside the caff is blummin huge. It nearly reaches the roof. I stand in front of it and look up at the lights. They ain't fairy lights, but normal light bulbs painted all different colours. It's got all these decorations too – red and purple and blue glass balls like bunches of grapes. It looks real pretty. There's rows of benches in front of it and I sit down for a bit to look at the tree.

There's a woman sitting on the bench in front of me and she's eating chips from a bag. I can smell them from where I'm sitting. I wish I'd bought some chips – I'm still pretty hungry. There's a bloke behind me with a big suitcase, reading a newspaper. I spect he's waiting for a train. I wish I had my suitcase with me and I was going somewhere nice. It'd be nice to be waiting here for a train and then getting on it and going somewhere nice. Like Scotland or somewhere.

There's loads of people coming and going. I spect they're coming home from work, cos they look like they're in a real hurry. There's some shops too and some people are going in to buy things – papers and books and that. I think about it for a bit, then I get up and go over to the shops. I like looking in shops – you know, not buying things, but just looking.

I'm just coming up to this shop when this girl stops me. I'm pretty surprised cos I don't know her. I hope she ain't going to ask me a question – you know, like where summat is, like the ladies or summat, cos to tell the truth I don't really know my way round here. But she don't ask me where nothing is, she just asks me if I can spare 10p. She needs some money for a ticket. I dunno if I got 10p, but I pull out my change anyhow. I hold it out to her so she can take 10p, and she takes the lot. I dunno how much it is – it's probably about 10p. She says thanks and then goes off. She don't look too well. She's young and that, but there's summat wrong with her eyes – they're all red and watery. I don't mind giving her money. I think it's a good idea to help people out if they ain't got money and that.

I don't go in the shop just yet. I stand outside and watch the girl going round asking other people for money. She's got a friend with her – a girl with long shiny hair like Marie's. Some people don't stop when she asks them for money, but

113

most people think for a bit and then dig in their pockets and give her summat. I reckon they must've nearly got enough for a ticket cos they ask quite a few people.

I get bored with watching them after a bit, so I go in the shop and have a look at their books. The shop ain't got no proper doors – it's just like part of the station so you can walk in and out without using a door.

Normally I like looking through books – you know, if they got nice pictures and that in them, but I dunno – I just ain't very interested at the moment. It's hard to concentrate on a book with all these people around. The shop's pretty crowded – I spect people are buying stuff for Christmas, so I just stand around watching them. Everyone seems in a real hurry, even when they're looking through books.

Then some music starts up. It's coming from outside, so I go out and have a look. There's this big brass band set up in the middle of the station with these people sitting in chairs with their instruments all silvery and shiny. It sounds really nice, the music they're making – it's all loud and echoey. They're playing Christmas songs – I know cos I heard this one at school before. We Wish you a Merry Christmas, this one's called. I go right up so I can see proper. They're all wearing the same sort of clothes – black, with these black hats – even the girls. I like the man who's playing this great big shiny thing like a fog horn. I listen real close to him, but he don't really play the tune – he just sort of goes blah-blah-blah every now and then. It don't really sound like the tune, but it fits in real well with the rest of them.

When they stop I give them a clap, but no one else does. Some people smile when they go past and there's this woman with a couple of kids over the other side from me, but most people just walk past like they ain't interested.

A girl in a smart black uniform is collecting money in this box and quite a few people stop and drop money in it. I wish I had some money to give her, but I ain't got none left.

The next song they play is a slow one – Silent Night. It's

one of my favourites. We used to sing this one at school. It's all about baby Jesus being born and that. I wish I could remember the words, but I've forgot them so I just hum along with the tune. It's nice that Jesus has got a birthday and that, just like a normal person. I like presents and all that, but – I dunno – if it's Jesus's birthday then why don't we give him prezzies? I know he's dead and that, but we could do things like, I dunno, like when you put flowers on someone's grave when they died. We could give little presents to Jesus, like flowers or summat.

The band plays for quite a bit. I know most of the songs, but there's one or two I don't. They're nice songs – even the ones I don't know. I specially like the man with the big silvery fog horn thing. I'd like to play one of them.

When they finish, the band pack up and fold their chairs up. There's lots of talking and laughing when they do that – they look like they've had a real good time. I just sort of hang round watching them. A big van pulls up and they stick their stuff inside and get in, but just before they go, the man with the fog horn thing turns round and says all friendly like, 'Happy Christmas'. I say 'Happy Christmas' back and then he gets into the van and they drive off.

It's real quiet after they've gone, and there ain't many people around. I really liked the band playing all them songs. It's a shame they had to go.

The shop's shut now. I think for a bit what I should do. To tell the truth, I could do with a pee, but I dunno where the toilet is. I spect there's one on the station somewhere, but I dunno where it is. I stop this man in a black uniform and ask him where it is, and he shows me. It's up the side of the platform – I can just see the light over the door from where I'm standing. I thank the man and go over to it.

The toilet's really big. It smells a bit, but it ain't too bad. I have a pee, then I wash my hands at the sink. You always got to wash your hands after you go to the toilet, cos there's germs and stuff. It's great, cos the water's warm, and I fill up the sink and keep my hands in it for a long time. My fingers feel all tingly, but it don't half feel good to stick them in the water. I look up at myself in the mirror while I'm soaking my hands. I keep forgetting I got my straw hat on. It's really neat I reckon – like that picture of the man in that rowing boat. Marie bought it for me, and she said it looked really great. She said I was a handsome devil, too. I smile at myself in the mirror.

I let the water out of the sink and dry my hands on this roller thing. It's busted, so there's a whole long sheet of towel on the floor, like a bog roll that's been dropped. It don't look too clean, but I dry my hands on it anyhow.

Back on the platform, I dunno which way to go. Sometimes I get like that, you know – I just forget where I am. Even in places I been to hundreds of times. Sometimes I forget people too, but not so often as places. I know I'm at the station, cos that's obvious, it's just I can't exactly remember how I got here. It's like I never been here before.

There's all these trolley things outside the toilet. They're sort of like cages and a car thing pulls them along, and stuff is stuck in them, like newspapers and all that. I know cos I seen them already. I walk right up to the end of the platform. There's a train in, but there ain't nobody on it, and all the lights are off. I been on a train with the school once – we went to the seaside and I cut my toe.

There's a sort of side bit with all these trolleys in, so I go in there. I dunno what the time is, but I reckon it's getting pretty late. I think it's about time I went back home. I can see this light shining from the side, so I squeeze through a couple of trolleys to see if I can get out that way. It ain't a door or nothing – it's just a big gap in the wall. I spect they use it for driving their vans through. But when I get there I can't find no way out. There's this sort of metal gate over it – you know, made of wire.

It don't look like there's no way out this way. I was hoping there was, cos it's about time I got back home – it's getting pretty late. I try and see where I can get out, but it's pretty dark where I am – I can't hardly see anything except these trolley things. I know the station's on one side, cos there's light coming from there, so I go back that way. When I get out, I'm going straight back home. But when I get to the other side I can't get onto the platform cos of this other gate. Suddenly I get all lost. I can't remember how I got in. I sort of start running now to find a way out quick, but this wire fence goes all the way down to the wall at the other end and I can't find no door in it. I wish it wasn't so dark. It's all confusing.

It's all crowded with all these trolleys and I keep bumping into them. I give my leg a nasty bash, but I don't stop and see if it's bleeding – I just want to get out. I just got to get out to where it's light. I try the other side again, but it's locked.

It's a horrible place. It's all dark and all I can see are these metal cages all round. I really want to get out of there. I look all the way round but all I can see are the shapes of the trolleys and the wire fence on both sides. If there was a light on I could find my way out easy, but it's too dark and confusing. All I want to do is get out.

I go back over to the other side. I'm so scared I start crying a bit. I keep banging into these horrible trolleys, and everything's all dark and dirty. There's a horrible smell like a garage, and I'm scared.

Then I see the way out. There's a gap in the wall, and it goes right onto the platform – there ain't no fence or nothing stopping me getting out. I'm real relieved when I see that, and head straight for the gap. I feel much better when I'm back on the platform, and I sit down for a breather. That was horrible in there, getting lost and that. I'm real glad to be out of that place.

It takes me a little time to get calm again. It was easy, really, getting out of there – it was just I was confused by it being dark and that. There wasn't nothing to be afraid of – it was only a side bit with some trolleys and stuff in it. But to tell the truth, I was pretty frightened.

I stand up and brush my coat down just in case it got dirty with me sitting on the ground. I think it's a good idea if I get back home now – I'm feeling pretty tired and

I want a lie down. I go back down the platform, back to where the shops are. One or two of them are still open, and it's still pretty bright with all their lights and that. There's a hamburger bar open, and it smells real good. I'd really like a hamburger, but I'm broke. I hope it don't take me too long to get home – I could do with summat to eat.

To tell the truth, I ain't really sure where I am. I know it's a train station and that, but I dunno how to get home from here. I just hope it ain't too far. I can see a policeman by the place they sell tickets. He's got his big winter coat on with silver buttons and his tall hat. They told us at school to ask a policeman if we got lost, and show him our yellow card with our name and address on it. I think for a bit about going to ask him how I get home but I don't want to ask him in case he tells Mr Jackson. If he told Mr Jackson then he'd come and take me to Combe Court, and I don't want that. And anyway, I ain't got my yellow card on me.

I hang around for a bit, pretending to look at some writing on the board. I could just ask him casual like – you know, like I'm going to meet a friend there or summat, but I can't remember the address. I'd know where I lived if I saw it, but just at the moment I can't remember the name of the street it's in, and the policeman wouldn't know if I don't have the address.

In the end I just walk past him without looking at him. I don't want him asking me questions like where I'm going and stuff like that, just in case he tells Mr Jackson. I don't think the policeman saw me. Even if he did, he ain't following me.

I dunno what to do now so I go up to the big electric sign board and have a look at it. It's got lots of words written up, one after the other – I suppose the names of where the trains are going. Sometimes there's a clicking noise and all the words change. It's pretty interesting watching that – the way the words change so quick.

There ain't many people about – I suppose cos there ain't no more trains. The platform's pretty empty. There's this man on this big white car thing going round cleaning the floor. There's sort of brushes under the car so when it goes round it sweeps and washes the floor at the same time. It looks pretty good fun, driving that thing. If I could get a job doing summat like that I reckon I wouldn't have to stay at Combe Court. When I got the job on the building site, Mr Jackson said I was grown up enough to live on my own.

I reckon I could do a job like that. It'd take me a while to learn how to drive it, but after I learned that I reckon I could do it. It don't look too hard, driving round and round. You just have to be careful not to hit anything.

I watch the man till he's finished and he drives off. The floor's all shiny and new looking now. It's empty except for this man and woman. They're looking up at the sign board, and holding each other's hand. I watch them for a bit. I spect the man's going away, cos they keep hugging and kissing like they do in films. I reckon that bloke's pretty lucky. I wish I had a girlfriend who'd hug and kiss me when I was going to catch a train. It must be real nice. He's much taller than the woman, and she sort of hangs from his neck when they kiss, stretching up on tiptoe to reach him. She can't stop kissing him. He's probably going away for a long time, that's why. It's sad, going away, but it must be nice all the same to have someone kiss you at the railway station.

I'm standing there watching them, and then suddenly they just walk off. They don't even go to the train place – they go the other way, and up the driveway and out of the station. I thought they was going to catch a train, and that's why they was hugging and kissing and that, but I dunno – maybe they was just planning to go away or summat. Anyhow, they just went.

Just then this voice comes over the loud speaker. I can't understand what the woman's saying – it's too loud and echoey to understand. It sounds sort of sing-song – not like someone talking at all, more like a tune. I dunno what she was saying. Probably stuff about trains and that. Someone blows a whistle, and this train starts rumbling, like it's getting ready to drive off. It's pretty smoky – the trains give off this browny smoke and it don't blow away – it just sort of drifts up to the roof. It looks pretty, but it smells flipping horrible.

I dunno what to do, so I go back to the caff and have a look in the window. It's nearly empty now. I think about it for a bit, then I go in. I ain't got no money, but I don't reckon they'll mind me sitting there and just looking out the window. It's pretty cold on the platform – I could do with getting warm.

I sit in the same seat as before, just by the window. No one comes up to me to ask what I want, so I reckon it's OK for me to be there. Someone's left a cup and saucer on the table, and when someone comes round, I pretend I'm drinking just in case they ask what I'm doing.

I dunno how long I sit there, but I reckon it's quite a while. I don't do much except look round and think about things – mostly Marie and that. It seems like ages since she's been gone. I reckon there'll be a letter from her now, cos she said she'd write to me. I got to get home though. I wish someone would come and take me home. I'm feeling pretty tired to tell the truth.

The same bloke who was there before comes up to me and tells me they're closing. He takes the cup off of the table and sticks it on his trolley.

I don't want to go out – it's blummin freezing outside, but I ain't got no choice. They're closing, so I got to get out. I put my hat on and get up.

I dunno how I'm going to get home. If I knew the way back, then I could walk, but I don't think I know the way from here.

I go and sit on the bench in front of the Christmas tree and stare at it. We had a big Christmas tree once – ages ago, it was. We stuck this white stuff like candyfloss on it – angel's hair it was called. Annie helped me put it on. She was only little then and I had to hold her up so she could reach. I pretended it was Annie's hair we was putting on the tree, and I called her a little angel, but she got upset about that, so I stopped. She was pretty touchy sometimes, Annie was. But she was a good kid really. She looked pretty as anything with her yellow hair and her cute little face. She was real clever too. She couldn't read or nothing cos she was too little, but she used to tell me stories – you know, made up ones like. When we finished decorating the tree, we stuck all the prezzies underneath and Annie told me what she reckoned they was. She was only guessing like, cos they were all wrapped up in paper, but she said she knew. She had a real good imagination, Annie did. I remember Mrs Seaton gave us some mince pies and we ate them hot, sitting on the floor in front of the tree – just the two of us. Annie told me I'd get a bike for Christmas – a red one with a basket. None of the prezzies was big enough for that, but she said it was a magic bike that got big when you wanted to ride on it.

Cos I'm thinking so much about Christmas and that, I don't see this old bloke till he calls out to me. He's sort of half-lying on the floor, holding onto one of the benches. I ain't sure if he's talking to me, so I don't say nothing.

'Give us a hand, son,' he calls out. 'My leg's come off.'

I get up and go over to him. He's pretty scruffy and I think he's spilt summat on his mac, cos there's a big stain down the front. His leg looks like it's broke – it's sticking out at a funny angle.

'Can I help you, sir?' I ask. I spect he's fallen over and can't get up.

'My leg's come off,' he says again. He leans forward and picks up one of his legs and pulls it right out from his trousers. I get a bit of a shock when I see that, cos it comes away from the rest of his body. Then I realise it's a false leg. I ain't never seen a false leg before. I know some people got them, but I ain't never seen one before.

'Help me get this back on,' he says, handing me the leg. Though he's old and that, he looks a bit embarrassed. His face don't go red or nothing, but he's got a sort of embarrassed look in his eyes. I spect it ain't very nice to have to ask people to help you with things like that.

121

Sometimes I get embarrassed if I can't do summat on my own. Sometimes you feel a bit stupid asking someone for a hand.

I look at the false leg for a bit while he pulls up his trouser leg. It's sort of creepy looking. It don't really look like a leg. It's the right shape and that, but it looks sort of artificial like a doll's leg, except big. It's made of plastic and it's all pink and shiny. It's supposed to look like skin, but it don't at all. It just looks like pink shiny plastic. It's blummin horrible I reckon. The foot is real enough, cos it's got this shoe and sock on it, but the leg bit is real creepy.

He tells me what to do, and shows me his stump. It's sort of bandaged up so you can't see the skin. I'm glad you can't see the skin, cos it's probably all shiny like Flora's hand when she got all her fingers burnt off. His leg comes to a sort of point, like the end of a pencil or summat and he tells me to shove it in the end of the false leg.

I don't mind helping him and that, but I must admit I'm feeling a bit uncomfortable with this leg.

'Push it on hard, son.'

I push as hard as I can. His leg sort of jams into the plastic like a pencil into a pencil sharpener. I help him get up and he stamps his leg so it goes on proper.

'God bless you, son,' he says, holding onto me. I think he's been drinking in the pub cos I can smell it on his breath. 'Tell me, are you a Jock?'

I dunno what he's going on about, so I just look at him.

'Are you from Scotland, like?'

'No, sir,' I say. He speaks a bit like Marie, so I suppose he lives in Scotland as well. He's swaying a bit and I have to grab him cos I think he's going to fall over.

'Well, maybe you've got Scottish ancestors then.'

He straightens up his mac and gives me a real serious look. Then he takes a bottle out of his pocket.

'Will you share a drop with me?' he says, waving the bottle so I can see it.

122

I think it's whisky or summat, so I say no thank you. I don't like whisky.

'All right then,' he says, putting it back in his pocket. 'God bless you, and a Happy New Year to you.'

He takes my hand and squeezes it hard. 'Are you sure you're not a Jock?'

He shakes his head like he can't understand summat, then he lets go of my hand. I'm glad he's let go, cos it was starting to hurt, he was squeezing so tight.

'Well, good night to you,' he says. He walks off and I watch him till he disappears round the corner. He walks funny – sort of dragging one leg, a bit like Fullblast. I spect it's cos he's got a false leg.

When he's gone, I think for a bit about Scotland. I suppose that's where he's from. I should've asked him if he knows Marie, cos that's where she lives now – in Scotland. I think about going after him and asking him, but I change my mind. He was friendly enough and that, but I dunno, I felt sort of uncomfortable with him. I couldn't really understand what he was going on about, and I didn't like the way he shook my hand so blummin hard.

I go back and sit on the bench by the Christmas tree. I wish I wasn't here. I wish I was back at home with Marie, and it was warm and we had summat nice to eat like fish and chips or summat nice like that. I have a look in my pockets to see if I got any sweets or anything, but I ain't. All I got is a ball of string and some bits of paper. I have a look at the paper to see what it is. It's that picture of a cat that used to be on Marie's wall. That was a nice picture – Marie liked it I think, cos she didn't mind me sticking it on the wall. It's a shame it's got ripped. It's gone right across its middle, but it don't matter too much, cos if you hold the bits together you can still see it OK. Looking at that picture reminds me of the photos of me and Marie – you know, them we took in that photo booth. I always carry them in my pocket – in the inside one, so they're safe and I won't lose them. I pull the pictures out and have a look at them. I always feel happy when I see them. It's hard

123

not to when you see how happy we are in the picture –
we're laughing our heads off. I dunno what was so funny,
but we was killing ourselves. I love these pictures – they're
my best things.

I really wish Marie wasn't in Scotland.

I get up after a bit and stick the stuff back in my pockets
and start walking the way I came in. I have to stop and let
a long line of trolleys go by. They rattle and bash into each
other, a whole long string of them. I spect they're being
taken someplace for stuff to be put in them. Most of the
platforms are empty, but there's a couple of trains still in.
Their engines are still on, rumbling like great big animals,
but I don't think they're going nowhere cos there's no one
about.

I get to the big entrance to the station and have a look
outside. I can see the lights from a couple of shops at the
end of the driveway, but they ain't open I think – they just
got their lights on. I dunno what's best – you know, if I
should go out or stay here. It's all dark and misty outside,
and it's real cold. I ain't really scared of the dark, not
normally, but looking out there, it's a bit scary. It looks
all big and open. There's all these buildings and streets
out there, but it's like they're all empty – you know, like
there's no one out there, just *things*. I know there's loads
of people really, it's just they're all at home asleep. But still
I get the feeling there ain't no one out there. It's all so big
and confusing – all them streets and cars and places.

I turn round and go back into the station. I dunno what I
want to do, but I don't want to go out there. At least I know
where things are in the station. I'd rather go home, but I
dunno how to get there, and I don't want to get lost.

They've switched the Christmas tree lights off, but apart
from that, the station's pretty light. The lights in the caff
are still on – it looks like it's open, but it ain't, cos I tried
the doors and they're locked.

I sit back down on the bench and sort of snuggle into my
coat to try and keep warm. I wish I still had my gloves – my
hands are freezing. I shut my eyes and try to go to sleep,

but there's too much going on to sleep. These vans keep coming and going and the man on the cleaning machine is having another go at cleaning the floor. It's too cold to sleep anyhow.

I watch this man with a red face and a little black hat sweeping all the rubbish up. There's loads of stuff round the benches and he makes quite a pile after a while. He sweeps under the bench I'm sitting on, and I lift up my feet so he can sweep under them. He don't say nothing to me – he just carries on sweeping like I ain't there. That looks a pretty good job, sweeping the floor, though I'd rather have a go on the sweeping machine. I suppose if you work at night you got to sleep during the day. Marie used to do that when I met her – you know, sleep all day and then go out at night. I suppose you get used to it after a while, sleeping in the day.

When the man finishes, he sticks all the rubbish in this big black placky bag like they have at the laundrette, and he takes it away. People leave a lot of litter around. They just chuck it on the floor. We was told at school not to do that. We had to find a proper bin to chuck it in. I think that's best, using a bin. If you just chuck it on the floor, then someone's got to come round after you and pick it up.

This man with long greasy hair and a sleeping bag sort of rolled into a ball comes over and starts looking in the bins. I dunno what he's looking for – maybe he lost summat. Sometimes you chuck summat away by accident and then you have to go looking in bins to find it. I don't think he finds what he's looking for, cos after he looks in all the bins he goes off without taking nothing out.

I think it's best if I get some sleep. I'm pretty tired now. I lie down on the bench and try and make myself comfy. I got to take my hat off, cos it keeps falling off and I don't want it to get dirty. Marie gave me that hat – I don't want it spoiled. I leave my shoes on, cos it's too cold otherwise. It ain't too uncomfortable, but it's really blummin cold. I wish I had my green sleeping bag with me, like that bloke before. I reckon I could sleep if I was warm enough.

125

I get a bit dizzy lying down on the bench, like I'm falling backwards and I got to sit up for a bit. I dunno if I'm feeling quite right. Things are looking a bit funny – you know, a bit dizzy-making. The roof's real high and all the noises are echoey. It's like there's nobody except for me – all alone in this big place, all open and cold.

Things are pretty busy now. They opened the gates by the steps and quite a few people are coming and going through them now. It was just a few at first, but after a while it got more and more till it's quite crowded now. The caff's open too. I thought about going in there, but I ain't got no money. I wish I'd got some cos I could really do with a hot drink. I ain't feeling all that well to tell the truth.

I suppose I got a bit of sleep last night. It's hard to tell, cos I always seemed to be awake, but then I remember waking up with a jump when this voice comes over the loud speaker. That was a bit of a shock, cos I was dreaming about summat about a train and Marie going away, and then suddenly I came to and found myself in the station. For a second I thought Marie was with me, but it was only a dream.

I'm real stiff from lying on the bench, so I get up and stretch. I stamp my feet to warm them up. My toes are froze – they're all sort of numb. I don't feel too tired, but I could do with summat to eat. I'm blummin starved.

I hang round the station a bit, watching the people all hurrying to catch their trains. Sometimes people are in so much of a hurry they run. I dunno why they're all hurrying. I don't understand that.

It's still dark outside. I expected it to be light, cos I thought it was morning on account of all the people all hurrying about. It's still misty as well. It ain't scary like it was before. It ain't scary when there's all these people around.

Some of the shops are open now. There's a caff down the road from the station with steamy windows and a couple of blokes in there having their breakfast. It looks real nice in there. I'd really like some breakfast. I got a nasty taste in my mouth – sort of stale like. I watch the two blokes through the window then I carry on walking. If I get home soon I can have summat to eat. I spect Marie's left some food in the cupboard.

The pavements and cars are all covered in this white frost sort of stuff. It looks pretty – all sort of sparkly like silver glitter or summat. I got to walk careful cos the pavements are so slippy. It's sort of like snow, but not quite. If you scrape your foot on the pavement you can make shiny black marks, like slugs make. The mist's real thick now. It makes everything look sort of fuzzy, and when cars drive past, their lights sort of fill up the street. It looks real beautiful.

It's like the mist's made everything all quiet. The traffic's real slow – the cars just sort of hissing past slow and quiet, their headlights all fuzzy and ghostlike. It's like walking in a dream, all the shops and cars and everything all sort of fairy tale, like they ain't really there. It's been dark for ages. Nights in winter are long – I dunno why, but they are. It makes me feel a bit funny being in the dark for so long. I dunno, but it ain't like normal, walking down the street with the lights all fuzzy. It's like it's still night and I never been to sleep at all.

Sometimes I get like I can't remember how I got some place. You know, it's like I'm suddenly there, just sort of plonked down in a place and I got to really struggle to remember how I got there. It's a bit like that walking down this street. I know I stayed the night at the station but it don't feel real. It's like it was someone else. It's a funny feeling.

It's still like nighttime, but I know it ain't cos there's too many people about. I spect they're all going to work or summat. They've been to bed and got up in the morning, and now they're going off and doing things, like going to work and that. It's always dark in morning in winter – it used to be dark when I got up to go to the building site.

127

It's morning and all that – it just looks like night.

Everything looks all quiet and special in the mist. It looks really nice – sort of misty.

I walk down the main road, past all these shops. I think I been here before, cos there's the telly shop from last night. The old woman's gone – I spect she's at home now. I stop a bit and watch a programme through the window. There's this woman talking to this bloke. I dunno what she's talking about cos I can't hear through the glass, but she keeps laughing at things he says. She looks all warm and comfy in her clean clothes and that. I wish I was in the warm. I'm aching all over.

I don't stay watching her too long cos I want to get back home, so I carry on down the road.

It's real busy now. There's all these hundreds of cars sliding past with their lights all red and white. Some cars have got yellow lights. One after the other, they're all pressed into one great snake. They're hardly moving at all – I can nearly keep up with them just by walking quick.

It's getting sort of light now. The street lights are still on, but the sky ain't black no more. It ain't sunny, it's just sort of grey. I ain't half glad that night's over, and it's going to be light soon. It ain't so misty now, but the pavements are still sparkly. With the light, it feels colder and I run down the road a bit to warm myself up. There ain't no shops or nothing round here. It's just a street and some old buildings – you know, for people to live in and that. It looks pretty nice now it ain't so dark. I'm real glad it's getting light.

There ain't a proper pavement here – it ain't concrete like, but just earth. There's sort of grass, but it's pretty wore out and it's mostly just mud, except hard. It feels like concrete on account of how cold it is, but it ain't – it's earth. There's trees too, all down the street. I like trees. They're better than lamp posts and that, cos trees grow out of the ground, so they're extra special like.

The street's real wide, and there's loads of cars jamming it up. There's loads and loads of cars here, all different. When I get to the end I stop and have a look round. I might have trouble crossing the road here. I got to be careful crossing the road, specially when I ain't feeling too good. But I'm lucky, cos there's this bloke who comes along, so when the lights turn green I just follow along behind him till I get to the other side.

I can see this park. I can't see too much of it, cos it's still dark, but it looks pretty big. It's got a pond, and there's all these trees. I think I'll go and have a look around. I like parks, specially when they got ponds, cos there's usually ducks and that. That'd be good fun, to go and watch the ducks. I wish I had some bread – I like feeding the ducks. I find some steps, so I go down into the park and have a wander round. The grass is all white and crunchy from the frost. Frost ain't good for plants, it turns them black and kills them off if you ain't careful, but I reckon grass must be OK. There's lots of trees and bushes. They're real nice – they ain't sort of usual trees, you know, like you'd find in a wood or summat. They look special – you know, all clipped and that. Not like wild trees at all.

I go down to the side of the pond to have a look round. I thought it might be frozen all over, like a picture I seen once with all these people skating on the ice, but it ain't. The sides are a bit icy and there's sort of puddles with sheets of ice over them. I step on a few and watch them crack in the middle like a sheet of glass. It's pretty good fun – I like the noise it makes when it breaks.

There's some ducks and that sheltering under some bushes. At first I couldn't see them, but when I heard a little quack I had a close look and saw them all there huddled together and trying to keep warm. It must be blummin cold for a duck in this weather. I dunno if they got nests or nothing to go to at night, but sat there under that bush all huddled up, they look froze to death. There's a sort of metal fence I can sit on, so I rest there for a bit and watch the ducks and that. They're all wrapped up

129

in their feathers like old men in blankets trying to keep warm.

It's a pretty nice park. It's got loads of flowerbeds and that, and a little bridge over the middle of the pond. It looks sort of like a picture – you know, a proper painting, with all the bushes and the frosty grass and that. If I was a real good painter or summat, I'd paint a picture of this all sort of dark green and grey and black.

I stay there for quite a bit, looking round and that, till it gets light. The sky sort of turns grey and then whitey-blue and then in the end it's daytime and it's all sunny. There ain't no clouds in the sky – just one or two wispy ones right above my head, but it's still blummin cold. It looks warm and that, cos it's so sunny, but it ain't warm at all. Maybe it's a bit warmer, but it ain't much. I don't really mind, cos it looks so nice in the sun, but I'd rather it wasn't so blummin cold. The ducks don't seem to mind it, cos there's quite a few swimming about now. There's all sorts of ducks here – all different colours. My favourites are these ones with black heads and a little red hat. It ain't a hat really, it just looks like one. They look real funny: they look sort of bad tempered and cross. A bit like Mrs Riley, to tell the truth. I wish I had some bread to give them; I spect they're hungry. I like watching them get out of the water – they look real funny. They sort of clamber out all clumsy like and then they waggle their tails like a dog and then start cleaning their feathers all quick. They look funny and cuddly – except for the geese. I don't really like the geese. They scare me a bit.

I wish I had a nice coat of feathers – my mac ain't all that warm, and my straw hat hardly keeps my head warm at all. They look sort of cosy in all their feathers. I suppose feathers must be pretty warm things.

I dunno, I'd quite like to stay watching the ducks, cos they're pretty interesting, but I'm too blummin cold for that and I got to get back home. I get up and start walking over to the bridge. There's a few people about now. There's this bloke with a white coat on and this bag of bread, feeding the birds. There's a load of pigeons round his feet, all fighting over the bits of bread he chucks them. I wish he would give me some of that, I'm flipping starved. The birds just sort of bob their heads like they're wind up toys. Then suddenly there's this loud bang from somewhere and they all fly off, like a mirror that's been smashed – pieces flying everywhere.

I sit down on the bench and look up at the sky. It really looks beautiful today – all blue and new and fresh. These white seagulls flash past, like flashing bits of light, and the traffic in the background rumbling away. It's like being at the sea, early in the morning with the seagulls and the sea pounding away and the fresh air. The old bloke's still chucking bread down. It's nice that he does that – you know, comes and feeds the birds like that. There's this baby starling with these funny stubby wings trying to get to bits of the bread but the other birds are too quick for it. I wish the old man would give some to it. I wish he would give me some too, but I suppose he brought the bread just for the birds.

It's too cold to sit around for long, so I get up and walk onto the bridge. It's a nice bridge, this. Half-way across there's this old pigeon just sitting on the side. It's all scruffy and wet and looks all beat up. It's just sitting there, not moving or nothing. We stare at each other for quite a bit – me and this pigeon. Its eyes are like glass beads – you know, like a toy's. It's hard to believe it can see anything with them eyes. They just look like bits of black glass. It looks so sad there, all cold and lonely, that I hold my hand out to sort of stroke it, but it flies off. I wasn't going to hurt it or nothing – I was just going to stroke it, but it flew off anyway.

I feel OK now. If I walk quick I don't feel too cold. I walk like I seen them soldiers do – the ones with the red suits and big hats I seen. They looked pretty good – all colourful and that, but I didn't stop too long to watch them. I dunno, but I didn't like the way the man was shouting at them. I dunno what he was shouting, but I didn't like it. He sounded angry. It was pretty good seeing them all marching together, though.

There's this blummin huge bridge so I stop a bit and look over the edge. The water's real black and cold-looking. I bet if you fell in there you'd get froze in a second. It's a long way down to the water but I can see a fag packet bobbing along. I spect someone chucked it off the bridge. It's like a little boat, bobbing there, up and down.

There's a couple of boats, but they ain't moving – they're just rocking side to side. I been on a boat once with the school. It was pretty good fun, but I felt a little sick from all the rocking.

I don't suppose it would matter much if I fell in anyhow, cos I can nearly swim. I can float and that, so if I fell in, that's what I'd do. I'd just lie on my back like Marie showed me and float like a fag packet. It'd be cold and that, but I wouldn't drown. One day I'll learn to swim real good, so I can go up to Scotland and show Marie and she'd be real surprised. She was a good swimmer in her blue swimsuit. I don't spect I could be as good as her, but I'd be nearly as good.

This long boat comes past and I run over so it goes underneath me. It's real wide and flat. It's got stuff in it, but I can't see what it is. I don't think it's a boat for people like the one we went on at school. I think it's for taking stuff to the factory and that.

When it goes past I want to run over to the other side of the bridge, but there's too much traffic to cross the road, so I just watch the trail of water it leaves behind. It's a sort of triangle, spreading further and further out till it reaches the sides of the river. That sets the little boats rocking like crazy, like there's a sudden storm or summat.

I try and find the fag packet, but I can't see it no more. Maybe it's sunk now – it was tiny compared to that boat. It's lucky I wasn't in the water then floating, cos that would've been dangerous with that boat going past. I have a look round for the fag packet, but it's gone. I spect it's sunk.

There's some seagulls floating on the water. At first I thought they was bits of paper or summat that someone chucked in, but when the big boat went past, they all flew off. It must be great to be a bird – you know, just flying over people and buildings and that. If I was a bird, I'd fly real high – as high as I could – close to the sun where I'd be warm. Then I'd just go round and round looking down on things – you know, like from a plane. Sometimes I'd come down to see people and do things, but only when I wanted to. If I was a bird, I'd fly to Scotland to see Marie. It'd be real easy – I'd just say to myself 'Well, I think I'll just pop over and see Marie today', and five minutes later I'd be there and we could have tea together, then if I didn't want to stay the night I'd just fly into the sky again and stay there. It never gets dark in the sky, so I'd never be afraid.

I stop outside this laundrette and warm myself up. There's all this steam coming out, sort of billowing out onto the street, and if I stand in it, it feels real warm. I'd like to go in for a bit, but there's loads of people in there and I ain't got no washing to do. But it's nice to stand out there in the warm steam, getting warm. I stay there for quite a while, until I get real good and warm.

If I nearly close my eyes and carry on walking I can pretend I'm blind. I seen a blind man once – he'd got a stick so he could tap the pavement so he didn't fall down no holes. I try walking for a bit with my eyes closed proper, but I keep having to open them cos I'm scared I'm going to bump into summat. If I was blind it'd be real difficult to go for walks and that. I suppose it'd be like nighttime all the time – you know, real dark and that, except you couldn't switch the light on.

I'm as hungry as anything. If I could have summat to eat, I'd have a big bowl of oxtail soup – all hot and steamy.

Like that time I was ill in bed. Oxtail soup and buttery toast and jelly for afters. Red jelly.

There's a sort of market here, like the one I used to go to with Marie and Sonja, cept not so big. It's mostly fruit and veg, but there's one or two stalls selling clothes and stuff. Socks and that. I'd like to buy a woolly hat – my ears are stinging, it's so cold, but I ain't got no money. I like my straw hat Marie bought me, but to tell the truth it ain't so warm as a woolly one.

I have a look in the gutter to see if any fruit or stuff has been chucked away. That's what I used to do with Marie – look for food they chucked away cos it was bashed up and that. Sometimes I got real nice things. I found a pineapple once. There wasn't nothing wrong with it – it was just a little bashed up on one end, that's all. I can't find nothing here, except a couple of old spuds, and they ain't no good cos you got to cook them first. I thought they was pears at first and I got excited, cos I like pears, but they wasn't. They're spuds.

It's only a little market, but the pavement's pretty crowded with all these people, and I keep getting bumped. There's this little bent old man with a shopping trolley thing and he bashes it into the back of my legs. He don't say sorry or nothing, even though he did it quite hard. He just goes on past me, puffing away and shoving this trolley thing in front of him. There's a stall selling chickens, all white and plucked with their heads cut off. Their skin's all bumpy, like they're cold, but they ain't of course cos they're dead. This woman with a red headscarf is looking at them and chatting to the man behind the stall. She's got a fag in her mouth, and she's squinting her eyes against the smoke. There's a long bit of ash on the end of her fag, and when she talks it falls off onto the chickens. Then she does summat that really shocks me. She grabs a hold of this duck's neck and starts twisting it – you know, like she's trying to kill it. She ain't looking at it – she's carrying on talking to the man, but she keeps twisting the neck of this white duck. I want to shout out and stop her, but I can't get no sound out. I can't believe it – you know, the way both of them are just being so normal like, and she's twisting the neck of this duck and killing it. Then I see what it really is, and I nearly laugh. It's a white placky bag she's twisting, not a duck's neck. It just looks like it. I really thought it was a duck.

I got to sit down after that, and I find a wooden crate. I'm sweating a bit, and my skin feels all prickly. I really thought it was a duck. I thought she was just standing there twisting the neck of this duck. It made me feel really funny seeing that.

It's real smoky and noisy with this traffic. I can feel the lorries every time they go past – the ground sort of shakes like a whatnot – an earthquake. There ain't so many people about, and them that are look like they're real busy – you know, just hurrying along as though they're in a rush to get home. I don't really like it round here – it's dirty and there ain't hardly any shops.

I'm feeling real heavy and tired and my feet's aching so I have a sit down on a wall and swing my legs for a bit. I dunno what to do – I really don't. I wish Marie was here – she'd know the best thing to do. She always knew what to do. I take out the photos of me and Marie and look at them. They've got bent from being in my pocket – there's a crease right across Marie's forehead. I sort of iron it out flat on my knee and look close. I remember when me and Marie took those pictures. We was in this railway station and Marie had just been to the dentist. I remember, I waited for her in the waiting room. After the dentist we went to the station to get the tube back to the house, and Marie said 'Let's get some photos for your swimming pass'. I remember I had to get some photos so I could get into the swimming pool for nothing. So I sat on this stool thing and Marie pulled the curtain and the light flashed twice and then Marie leaps in and sits on my lap, and it flashes again. I couldn't wait for the pictures

135

to come out, I was so excited to see them. And when we seen them, we just bust ourselves laughing, cos they looked so funny with Marie's hair all over the place and me with this real surprised look on my face.

I wish I could find my way back home. It can't be far, I know that, but I dunno the way. If I had the address on a yellow card I could show it to someone and they'd tell me. They'd say 'Oh yes, I know. Down this road, turn this way and then turn that way and you'll be there. It ain't far.' I'd thank them and I'd be home in five minutes and I could sit in Peter's room looking at his stuff and chatting with him. It'd only take a minute to get back and then all this would be over. But I got to carry on walking, cos I don't have no card. Maybe if I walk long enough I'll get to Scotland and I can see Marie. She'd be real surprised to see me, I bet.

Then I get a real good idea. Bayswater! Billy Bayswater! That's where I live! I'm so pleased with myself I shout it out. Bayswater! It ain't a street or nothing, but if I get there I might recognise summat and then know where I am. Then I could find the house and unlock the front door and go in and everything. I'm real chuffed with myself for thinking of that. That was a real grown-up thing to do.

There's a woman just up the road so I hop off the wall and run after her. My legs are a bit wobbly and I nearly fall over. I steady myself against the wall. I mustn't get too excited, but I can't help it – I'm going to be back home soon and everything's going to be OK.

The woman's dark like runny chocolate, her skin all smooth and beautiful. She's heard of Bayswater and she points up the road. You'll have to go back into town, she says. I'm so pleased with her for knowing the way I want to hug her. I don't, cos it ain't polite with strangers, but I give her a real nice smile instead. She smiles back at me, all sort of friendly. She ain't young or nothing – I spect she's got kids and that, but her skin is so lovely and soft-looking and warm like runny chocolate I just want to touch it. I don't – I just say thank you and goodbye, then I go off up the road. God, I'm so happy I could dance!

Now I know the way I don't feel tired no more. Sometimes I get a little dizzy and that and I sort of feel real tall – you know, like a giant. When I look down at my feet they look miles away. I feel OK and that, but just a little funny. I don't mind though – I'm going to be home soon. I got to remember the name so I don't forget. Bayswater. Billy Bayswater.

I walk as quick as I can, till I'm nearly running. It's great to be out somewhere and then decide to go home, and there it is, waiting for you, and all you got to do is walk a bit and then you'll be home and everything'll be OK. I'm looking forward to having summat to eat, and then having a lie down. I'd quite like a rest now, and I would if there was somewhere to lie down, but I don't want to get dirty. I'm feeling a bit dizzy to tell the truth. I'm feeling OK and that, but just a bit dizzy.

There's a house with a broken window – a big black hole in the window, and I laugh at it. I'm going home. I don't have to stay here. I got my own home and it ain't got a broken window. It's got an electric fire and food in the cupboards, and I got a cat and a sleeping bag and all sorts. I'm better than any old broken window.

If I had a broken window I wouldn't put my fingers through it – no way. That'd be stupid. What I'd do is stay on the other side of the room so I wouldn't get sucked through it. They're dangerous, broken windows. I hurry on past – I don't want to put my fingers through the glass.

It's getting dark. I didn't know, but then suddenly the street lights come on. I stop under a lamppost and look up at the light, all orange and flickery. Then I get this hot feeling at the back of my head and everything goes funny and I find myself on the floor. I've fell over. I felt so dizzy looking up that I fell over. I sort of get up onto my knees and breathe for a bit. I still feel a bit odd – there's these red flashes of light and all these patterns in front of my eyes, and I sort of feel hot and cold at the same time. Everything looks all far away and all lit up in the street lights. I hope I ain't going to have a fit. Marie would be disappointed. I got to take it easy and not get too excited, or else I might have a fit. I stay there a bit, sort of squatting down, trying not to feel too dizzy.

I love Marie – I really do. Did I say that before? I can't remember, but it's true. I love Marie like I love Annie. They're my two best people. One day we'll all live together and we'll look after each other. I can help Annie with things, like getting things she can't reach or cutting up her food, and she can tell me stories, and Marie'll sit by the fire just looking pretty and we'll never go out or nothing, but stay in all the time, just the three of us. And we can have a dog and a cat – Simon and Satan. And nobody won't take them away from us, cos we'll be grown up like a proper family.

I stand up and lean against the lamppost for a bit, till I stop feeling dizzy. I mustn't get too excited. I got to be grown up and remember where I'm going to.

I'm doing pretty well I reckon. This man told me I had to go over the bridge, and here I am. I stop in the middle of it and have a look round. It's too dark to see much of the water. I can just see these winking lights underneath me. Most are just white, but some of them are coloured, like. It's real dark now, like nighttime, and I can see all the lights of the city all lit up. It looks real pretty, all them lights. There's buildings on both sides of the river, all lit up. It looks like a fairy land – all special and pretty like Christmas. I wish Annie was here so I could show her. She'd like this, how all the buildings look so special with their lights on.

I spect I'll be home soon. I still dunno where I am, not really. But I don't reckon it's far, cos I been walking for ages. My legs are aching like mad now, but I don't stop to have a sit down or nothing. I keep on walking, cos Marie'll be waiting up for me. I spect she's worried about me, being gone so long. But I bet she'll be real surprised to see me. And proud too, cos blimey, I been walking for ages and when I get back home she'll think I been real clever to find my own way back, and I ain't got a yellow card or nothing.

The pavement feels a bit springy. I dunno if it's cos it's new, but it feels spongy. It's weird walking on it – I can feel my feet sink into it like I'm walking on rubber. If I get too tired I might just have a lie down and have a little kip. I'm pretty warm so I don't need a blanket or nothing and I can just bunch up the pavement into a pillow if I need one. I reckon that'd be just as comfy as a proper bed. It feels real soft and warm. And if anyone came up and told me off for sleeping on the pavement I'd say I was the King of England and I can sleep anywhere I like.

But I don't lie down – I just carry on walking. I got to be careful of the traffic, cos a car nearly hit me. This man stopped real quick and blew his horn and shouted summat at me. I didn't hear what he shouted, but I was pretty lucky I wasn't run over, cos to tell the truth I wasn't really looking where I was going. I was looking in all the shop windows, at the reflections. I got to be more careful and watch where I'm walking. I don't want to have an accident.

Once I seen someone dive into the road like diving into water. They just went in head first and was swallowed up in the road. It wasn't as splashy as water – it was sort of like cake mix. Sort of poury like but not too wet. They didn't come up again – I dunno where they went. I dunno why I thought of that – I just did.

Why didn't they come and visit me, Mum and Dad? Everyone else had visitors – cept for Captain. I really wanted them to visit me, but they never did.

*

Sometimes I think about things we do – you know, everyday things like walking or washing our face or eating or summat. Sometimes when I think about them, they seem real complicated. Like if you thought about how you walk – you know, moving your legs and all that – it's real hard. I try it for a bit, thinking real hard about walking. I walk real slow, feeling my body all heavy, like I got big boots on. I suppose when babies learn to walk it's like this – you know, one foot in front of the other real slow and wobbly. I try walking like that for a bit. I dunno why, I just do. I suppose it's interesting. People don't know how hard walking is when you really think about it. I'm surprised how clever people are, walking without even thinking about it. It's pretty amazing the way we can do all these things. Sometimes we just don't think about how clever we really are.

I get this big feeling again. It's like everything's a long way away, and everything's real big and unreal looking. It ain't scary or nothing – it feels quite good, sort of like a dream. Maybe I *am* dreaming.

It's real busy here. There's loads of shops with their lights on and traffic and people hurrying along the pavement. I'm still walking real slow. I ain't trying to, it's just I can't walk quick. It's like I'm real light – you know, like one of them silver balloons – and every step I have to be careful not to float off. I think about my legs, but I don't really have no feeling in them. I can still make them work and that, it's just like they ain't mine. You know, it's like that plastic leg I saw once – you know, the false one.

I don't really mind this walking. It's easy enough and it's pretty interesting. What I don't like is the noise. Everything's so loud. I go past this bloke selling papers and he shouts summat out and I got to stick my fingers in my ears, it's so loud. His shouting sounds like a trumpet or summat. It should be a nice sound, but it's too loud and it sort of upsets me. The cars are all blowing their horns too. I really don't like that. It ain't that it's too noisy –

it's just, you know, like a dentist's drill or summat – it's a noise that makes you want to run away from it.

I try walking with my hands over my ears, and it's a bit better. I can still hear stuff, but it sounds swishy like when you listen to one of them curly sea shells. It's like I'm just floating down the street, just a head bobbing along in the water. Sometimes I think I'm invisible and I can pour myself into places like I'm made of water. Invisible water just running over things, round people, down the street. Warm water running away, and nobody can't see me and nobody can't catch me.

I'm happy now. I'm warm and free and there's lights and people, and nobody's asking me questions. Nobody can't catch me cos I'm invisible. They can't see me. I'm just water swirling round them and they're too busy to feel me. They can't feel me cos they don't know I'm there, and if I want to I can fly over their heads and leave them behind and live in the sky. So I dance. I dance like I'm splashing water, swirling round them, down the street. Everything's so bright and beautiful and nobody can't see it. They're all statues and I'm dancing into the gaps between them, rolling into the spaces like I'm a ball of water – a red watery marble rolling along the street and nobody can't see me and nobody can't catch me.

I could walk like this for ever. Just roll down the street, going on and on and on. The lights are like smashed glass – all shattered into a million bits. I stop and watch the traffic lights change. Red, orange, green – they sort of fill me up with colours. Red, orange, green – I could stay here forever.

It's her! It's Annie! She's walking along the pavement ahead of me, holding onto this woman's hand. I dunno who the woman is, but it's Annie. She's had her hair cut, but it's Annie all right. I run after her, bumping against people in my rush. God, she'll be surprised to see me! I get stuck in a crowd of people coming out the tube and

I have to stand on tiptoe so I can keep my eye on her. I shout 'Annie!' but she don't hear me. I'm laughing like crazy – I can't believe it. Annie, come to see me! There's a gap in the crowd and I dart through and run after them. I call out her name again, but she still don't hear me – she's too busy talking to the woman. She's got this cute little duffle coat on and a bobble hat with her hair sticking out the bottom. I overtake them and turn round. 'Annie,' I say, squatting down like I used to. She'd always run into my arms when I did that so I could lift her up, but she don't do it this time. They stop, Annie and the woman, and just stare at me. Then I see it ain't Annie – it ain't her at all. It's some other little girl. I feel real weird all of a sudden, seeing it ain't Annie. I just stay there, squatting down and the woman gives me a funny look and tugs the little girl's hand and they walk round me and go off down the road. I turn and watch them go. I thought it was Annie – I really did. She had the same colour hair, all yellow and curly, and she walked in just the same way, sort of little bouncing steps.

I just stay there, squatting on the pavement, blubbering like a baby. I thought it was Annie, and we'd go home together and see Marie and they'd both be proud of me and we could sit in front of the Christmas tree together and guess what the wrapped up presents were, and eat mince pies and all that. I was sure it was Annie, but it wasn't. I made a mistake, and I'm so stupid. Nobody won't come and see me cos I'm so stupid and I always make mistakes. And Mum's always telling me off for doing things wrong. That's why they sent me to school – cos I'm handicapped. Now nobody's going to come and see me, and Marie's gone away and Annie don't know where I am and they won't have Christmas with me and we won't open prezzies together.

It's just colours I can see through my tears – just smashed bits of colour. I don't want to go on. I'm too tired. I just want to stay here and sleep. I'm warm and tired and the ground's soft, so I just lie down where I am and shut my eyes. The noises swirl round me, but it don't bother me.

I'm falling. Falling head over heels in black. I won't move. I won't move for ever. They left me at school, Mum and Dad and Annie. They took me there in the car. Simon was in the back on his tartan rug and he kept licking my suitcase. I didn't know where I was going and I was scared. Annie had drawed me a going-away card – a real good picture of a man and a house. I couldn't really tell what it was till she told me, but when she did I could see it. It was a real good card. I had that in my hand and I was crying. Mum and Dad were all tight and not saying much and Annie just chatted away to me in the back and Simon kept licking at the suitcase like it was a bone or summat. And then we got to school and it was all big and confusing and there was all these boys I'd never seen before, all with their parents and some of the kids were weird-looking with funny eyes. One kid was in a wheelchair and this other one couldn't walk proper. I didn't want to stay there – I wanted to go home, but Mum told this old woman my name who smiled at me and showed me my bed and that. Mum helped me put my clothes in the drawer. She said I'd have a real good time here – playing sports and sleeping in the dorm with all the other boys. I tried to believe her, but I was too scared. I really didn't want to stay there, even if we did play sports and everything. There was this funny smell and all these strange kids. They all knew each other and was laughing and kidding around and I was scared cos it smelt so bad and was so big and bright and I didn't know where I was. Then Mum and Dad and Annie all said goodbye and I was crying and so was Annie. Dad patted me on the head and Mum gives me this little kiss on the cheek and then they went off and left me with this old woman. Mum kept calling her 'sister', but she wasn't my sister – Annie was and I didn't want to stay there, but they went off and left me.

I open my eyes and push myself up. I dunno what I'm doing lying on the floor, getting all dirty. I stand up and brush my coat down. My hat's fell off so I stick it back on and look round. I feel OK now – it's just my legs are aching. I ain't had a fit or nothing – I was just lying down cos I was tired. I stand there a bit, organising myself. I got to get back home, that's the thing. I got to be grown up and ask people the way. I stop this man and ask him where Bayswater is, but he don't understand me and just shrugs. Then I see a policeman and I go over to him. The policeman knows OK and tells me, but he looks at me funny all the time. He asks if I'm all right and I say yes. I don't feel too bad – my legs ache and I got a sort of tight feeling in my tummy, but apart from that I'm OK. It's a little complicated what he says, and I don't follow it all, but I know he said carry straight on down this street, so I thank him and go off. That's what they told us to do at school – ask a policeman if we're lost.

The street goes on for ages, but it's pretty interesting. There's loads of shops I can look in and there's all these Christmas lights. It's real pretty. I'm glad it's Christmas and there's lights in the shop windows and all that. When I get home I'll make Marie and Annie a Christmas card. I'll do a real nice one and get Peter to write inside it so it's all neat. I'll do that tomorrow when I'm home.

At the end of the street, there's this big square with loads of people in it. It's like this film I seen about these penguins – you know, how they all lived together on this island, and they was loads of them, all jammed together. In the middle of the square there's this huge Christmas tree. I never seen a Christmas tree so big – it's as high as a house. It's got all these white lights all over it and it's real tall. It looks great there, standing in the middle of the square, looking down at all the people and cars and that. It's even bigger than the buses that go past.

There's a man cooking chestnuts on the corner and I stop and warm my hands over the fire and look at the Christmas tree. The chestnuts smell real good – all hot and nutty. I'd really like some, but I ain't got no money, so I just make do with warming my hands. Everything looks real pretty round here – the lights and the tree and the stalls selling postcards with their lights on. It feels real Christmassy – you know, all sparkly and glittery and that.

There's a lot of traffic here and it takes me quite a bit to cross all the roads to get to where I want. I dunno, but I get the feeling everyone's all looking forward to Christmas – you know, opening all the prezzies and stuff like that. A couple of girls go past and they got this red sparkly stuff wrapped round their necks – you know, a sort of silvery string they hang on Christmas trees. I spect they've been to a party. They look all happy and warm together, wrapped up in their winter coats with this sparkly stuff round their necks like a scarf. I call out 'Happy Christmas' after them, but they don't hear.

My ears are burning in the cold, but there's nothing I can do about it. My fingers are froze too. They don't work so well on account of how swollen they are – they're all sort of purply and itchy. I try rubbing them, but I'm too tired to do that for long, so I just stick them back in my pockets.

I get a bit dizzy again and have to take it easy, so what I do is I walk with one arm against the shop windows and that, so I don't fall over. I can't walk too quick like that, but at least I don't fall over.

There's this shop, all lit up with these bright lights, and loads of stuff in the window – toys and that. I stop in front of the shop and look inside with my forehead sort of pressed against the glass. There's these springy sort of things bouncing up and down on a string like they're alive. They look like some sort of animal, bouncing up and down like that. I watch them for quite a while. They just go up and down, up and down and never stop. My eyes go funny after a bit, so I look at summat else. There's this red Father Christmas – a sort of plastic doll thing. It looks pretty weird. I think it's a blow-up thing – you know, like a rubber ring you go swimming with. It don't look like a

Father Christmas much, but I know it is, cos it's got a red suit and a white beard. I don't like its eyes. They're just sort of painted on – you know, like black dots. I wouldn't really fancy that – it'd be no good to cuddle or nothing. It's too shiny and that.

There's this siren going behind me, getting louder and louder, and I turn round to have a look. It's a big white ambulance with a blue light on top, flashing on and off. It's making a hell of a racket, but it stops the noise after a bit, cos it gets stuck in the traffic. I don't like noise that loud. It upsets me. I turn back and carry on looking in the window, but it's hard to concentrate with this blue light flashing on and off in the glass. On and off. Blue and then nothing, real quick. It's like it's flashing in my head. I shut my eyes, but it's too late. I can see all these sparks and flashes – red and blue fireworks going off. Then I feel myself falling.

My teeth are soft like chewing gum. I bite them together and feel them squash. My head hurts real bad – right inside my eyes. I sit up and rest against the wall. It hurts too much to keep my eyes open, so I just sit there trying to concentrate. I had a fit – I know that. My legs are warm and I give them a feel. I think I wet myself. I open my eyes and try and look at my trousers to see if it's true, but my eyes are all blurry and I can't see proper. I hope I ain't wet myself.

It takes me a bit to remember where I am. It's pretty confusing at first, cos all I remember is this blue light, and it ain't here no more. At first I thought I was out shopping with Marie, cos of all the people and cars and that, but then I remember I'm lost. I'd like to stay lying down for a bit to make my headache go away, but I made a puddle on the pavement and I got to move. I get up and lean against the window and sort of pat down my coat. I'm all embarrassed cos my mac's all wet with the pee. There's a big warm patch on the back. My trousers and socks are wet too. It's real embarrassing to wet yourself.

People think you're a baby. I wish I didn't have fits. I hate wetting myself like a baby.

I got to carry on. I got to find Marie and get my trousers changed. I hope she ain't far cos I really want to change my trousers and take off my mac. It's stupid to wet yourself like a baby. I want to go home. I really do.

I stop these couple of young kids and ask them where my home is, but they just laugh at me. They don't go off or nothing – they just stand there laughing like summat's real funny. I dunno what they're laughing at, but I smile like I understand. My head still hurts real bad, and I'm still a bit confused, but I pretend I understand. I say thank you, and carry on. I dunno if they told me the way – I can't remember, but I think it's this way.

Walking's real difficult now, and I have to stop every now and then to steady myself against a wall or a lamppost. My legs feel real heavy. The people walking past look like puppets, moving all quick and jerky. All the traffic looks shiny like it's just rained, or they all been polished. It looks kind of nice, but I don't stop and watch it. I dunno, but there's summat scary about the cars and that. It's like they're sharks or summat, or fish with these big white eyes looking for things to eat. And they're real dangerous too – they might jump onto the pavement and swallow me up with their big eyes. I don't want to go near them, so I walk right up against the shops, sort of leaning right against the windows so they won't get me.

It's so bright and noisy. I dunno where I am. It's like a fairground. Maybe that's it. All these kids and lights and noise, and it's sort of scary and exciting at the same time. I dunno what all these people are doing. Maybe summat special is happening and they're rushing to get there, cos they look real excited and busy and hurrying to get some place. But their eyes scare me, how shiny they are. And they don't look – you know, like they ain't really seeing. Like a doll's eyes, or a pigeon's eyes. They just rush on by.

I want to shut out the noise. It's too much. I want to

put my hands over my ears, but I'm too tired. I'm really, really tired. Even if there was a fair I wouldn't go. I just want to go to bed and get to sleep.

I got to be careful at the doorways, cos there's people coming in and out and a couple of times I nearly get knocked over by people bumping into me. There's this doorway with no light on and I trip over summat and have to grab a hold of the side. My head's spinning, so I just sort of lean there a bit and have a rest. Summat's moving on the floor and I sort of watch it out the corner of my eye. It's a dog I think, chewing on a bone or summat. I'd give it a pat if I had the strength, cos I really like dogs, but I just turn my head and look at it instead. Then I see it ain't a dog – it's a person. They're all wrapped up in bits of cloth and lying on all this cardboard. It's a woman I think – a young black woman with a woolly hat on. She don't say nothing to me, she just looks at me with these big eyes. Her look's kind of scary – I seen people at Combe Court like that. They're the ones that's always shouting and chucking things and causing trouble. I dunno why she's lying there. Maybe she's ill or summat. But I don't understand why she don't go home instead of lying on that cardboard. It must be pretty uncomfortable sleeping like that, and I bet it's cold without no proper blankets and stuff like that. I don't say nothing to her – I just stare at her a bit. I know it ain't polite to stare, but she's doing it to me, and to tell the truth I'm so tired I can't move. She looks like an animal lying down there. Not a dog or nothing, you know, not an animal you keep in the house, but one in the wild, like a fox or summat. It's like a little cave in there in the dark with her rags and her bits of cardboard – like a cave and she's an animal who lives there and is all scared and angry when someone comes in by accident. I say I'm sorry for treading on her, but she just looks at me like she don't understand. Maybe she's deaf or summat. I turn round and go back onto the street and then have one last look at her. She ain't moved. She's still staring at me like an animal.

*

I dunno where all these people are going to. Maybe they know summat cos they all look like they know where they're going. All these faces sliding past me, all lit up in the light – it's like a dream. All these faces. Annie and Marie. Mrs Seaton. And Mum.

Why didn't she come and visit me? Why not? I wanted her to come and she never did. She never did.

I must've spilt summat or maybe I trod in a puddle cos my trousers are all wet and cold. I dunno where I am. I think I'm going some place but I can't remember where. Maybe I'm going to meet Marie – I can't remember.

The pavement's too crowded to walk on without bumping into people, so I step off and walk in the gutter. There's all these people. Hundreds and hundreds of them, and none of them know me. All these hundreds of people with shiny eyes and they're all going home.

I've fell over again – I just can't stay on my feet. It didn't hurt when I fell over cos the road's real soft and spongy. Everything looks so high from here, and I'm all squashed and thin like I'm paper and people can walk over me and it wouldn't hurt and they wouldn't know I was there. There's a fag end on the ground by my eye and I watch it for a bit. Someone's chucked it down there and they've gone off and forgot it and they don't even know who I am. They've just gone off somewhere and left it behind.

I'd like to stay here on the floor but there's cars beeping at me and I think I'm lying in the road, so I push myself up and sort of crawl to the pavement. There's some people standing round watching me, but they don't give me a hand. They just stand there looking at me. When I get onto the pavement I just sit there with my feet in the road. I don't feel too good. I feel sort of sick. Suddenly I start puking into the road, but nothing comes up except this slimy stuff. It tastes horrible and I spit it out. I puke again, but it's just like my tummy's being squeezed and all I do is make this coughing noise and nothing comes out.

My eyes feel all hot and my head's prickly like someone's pulled my hair.

I sit there for quite a bit, hunched up on the pavement. I'm blummin freezing now – I can't stop shivering. My teeth are chattering like mad. I wish someone would come along and take me home.

My hat ain't on my head, and I look round for it. I can't see it nowhere – it must have fell off someplace. I'm real disappointed about that. It was a nice hat, and Marie gave it to me, so it's extra special. I feel on my head again, but it ain't there. She bought that for me, Marie did, and now I've gone and lost it.

I dunno how long I sit there, I just sit there and sort of watch the cars go by. I'm still shivering, but I don't puke up again. I'm a bit dizzy when I stand up and have to hang onto this litter bin, but I'm OK after a bit. I carry on walking down the street, careful not to bump into people so I don't fall over again. Sometimes I got to stop and breathe deep cos I feel sick, but I don't puke up again.

I don't understand. There's this bloke on top of this bus – you know, one of them big ones with no roof, and he's just shouting. I can't understand what he's saying, but he's just shouting at the lights and everything, like he's real angry about summat. The bus turns the corner and it gets stuck in some traffic for a bit and he just carries on shouting again and again. I dunno why, but he is. Again and again. He's sort of waving one arm and hanging on with the other. I dunno. I just dunno.

It's like a bath, stepping into a hot bath of all these colours. There's lights all across the road, from one side to the other. Big stars and a Father Christmas and reindeer and it's all so bright just hanging over my head and stretching all down the road like a tunnel of hot colour all hanging in the sky so beautiful and magic. I can't believe it. I ain't never seen anything like it – all them colours and Father Christmas, huge, as big as a giant – all red and gold and glittery. It's the most beautiful thing I ever seen. And stretching all down the road, hundreds, millions of lights and colours. I can't stop myself from laughing and clapping my hands. This is where I been going to. It's like church with the sun shining through them coloured windows and pictures of Jesus with light all round and angels floating in the sky and the sun shining and all that. It just falls all over, all round me like a firework going off and floating down the sky.

I wish Marie and Annie was here so they could see it. I look round for someone to show it to. There's this man and woman walking by with lots of shopping bags and a little boy hanging on to his Dad's belt.

'Look!' I shout, pointing into the sky.

They all glance up quick and then back at me. I say it again and the man looks at me a bit angry like. I squat down next to the little kid and point again.

'Look at the lights!'

He looks scared of me, and hangs even tighter on to his Dad's belt. His Mum sort of turns him away and says summat foreign and they all walk off quick.

I try someone else, but they don't stop. This old woman don't hear the first time, and when I say it again, she just says yes and walks away. She just walks away. I mean, she don't even look up at the lights. Why don't they look? Why don't people see how beautiful it is? I don't understand.

The people slide past like fish and I'm sucked down the street, heading for the next and then the next set of lights. When I'm under them, it's like standing in the sun. It's all hot and bright and lovely. And then the next lot of lights sucks me to it and I just slide down the street. I'm just slipping down the hill being bumped by people but I don't hardly notice. All there is, is this colour and more of it and more of it.

Then the lights just stop. At the bottom of the hill,

they just stop and it's a normal street. I turn round and look back. When I do that, it's like summat inside of me is pulled out and streaks back up the street, under all the lights, right round the corner to where I can't see. I got to shut my eyes and turn round. It's too beautiful to look at.

I carry on walking. I don't look back or nothing. It's so beautiful it's sort of scary – you know, feeling so excited at the lights. But I wish Marie and Annie had seen them lights. They would've understood. They would've looked at the lights, I know. But it's too late now. They won't never see it. They won't never know how beautiful it was.

It's just a normal shop window – you know, with lights on and these statues and that, but it's been done like it's someone's dining room. There's a little pretend fire with red light flickering and a real Christmas tree with little fairy lights and stuff hanging from it. There's prez-zies all wrapped up under the tree, just like we used to have when I lived with Annie and Mum and Dad. There's this big table with these people sat round it like they're having dinner – Mum, Dad and a little girl. She ain't really the same as Annie. Annie's much more pretty, but it's sort of like her – you know, about the same size and that. They're all sitting round this table, like they're going to start eating any moment. There's a wicker basket in the middle of the table and plates and glasses and stuff on the table. I can see a bottle poking out the basket and there's a chicken too, all brown and cooked. They're only statues – I know that – but they look really real, just like a real family sitting round a table just about to eat their Christmas lunch.

I stand looking in that window for ages. I'd really like to be in there. They all look so happy and warm like a real family, just like Annie and Mum and Dad. I have a look round to see if Simon's there, but I can't see him. Mum never lets Simon in the room when we're eating, so that's why. He's probably locked in the kitchen, scratching at the door trying to get out. I wish Marie was here to see them. She'd be real surprised to see them all sat round the table looking so happy.

I got my nose pressed against the glass and it keeps steaming up with my huff, so I wipe it with my fingers. I wish I was in there. I wish I could sit at the table and help cut up Annie's food like I used to, and we'd have crackers and we'd wear those paper hats and have them little prezzies from inside the crackers. And if I got summat Annie wanted – you know, like a little necklace or a whistle or summat, I'd just give it to her, and Mum would say what a polite boy I was, and Dad would smile at me, and we'd all be happy. I spect Mrs Seaton's still in the kitchen. She's probably heating up the mince pies so we can have them hot when we're sitting on the floor in front of the Christmas tree trying to guess what the wrapped up prezzies are.

The window keeps getting misty and I have to rub it so I can see through. I wish they'd let me in. I wish they would. Annie's going to be in bed soon, and I ain't said goodnight to her. Dad's going to carry her upstairs and tuck her into bed with her bunny hot water bottle, and leave her light on so she don't get scared in the dark.

I wish this window wouldn't keep getting steamy. I rub it real hard. It's making me annoyed. They shouldn't have left me at school. I didn't want to stay there and I didn't want to go to Combe Court, cos I hate it and it smells and the Captain slobbers in his food and Christmas is horrible with no good prezzies and Annie not there. Why didn't you visit me? Why not? Why did Marie go away? Why did she leave me like that? Now I got no one. I want to go home. I don't want to stay out here. I know I'm shouting, but I don't care if I'm being naughty. I want to go home.

I bang on the glass with my fist. Soft and then harder and harder. I want to break the glass, but it's too thick. I can't get in. I start screaming and chucking myself against the window, but it won't break. They won't let me in. I run fast as I can at the window, but it still won't break. It won't break. There's a red smear on the window. I can taste blood running down the back of my throat, then my arms are grabbed and everything just spins all colours and then black.

My fingers don't work too well. They all wrapped up in white bandage stuff. I think they're my fingers, but it's hard to tell. I'm in bed with this blue blanket and my feet sticking up. A girl's sitting next to me. It's big here, like school. My fingers are all white. I'm warm and sleepy and there's this girl. I dunno who she is.

'One more mouthful, then we're finished.'

I dunno who this girl is. She's wearing a white dress. I think she might be a nurse, but I dunno where I am.

'Come on, Billy.'

She's holding a spoon. I look at her face. She's got pretty eyes. Like a cat's with the sun shining in them. I like her eyes. They're real pretty.

'Open your mouth, Billy.'

My fingers are all bandaged up. I must have hurt them, I reckon. The girl pops a spoon in my mouth, and then scrapes at my chin.

'There's a good boy.'

There's a girl sitting next to me. I dunno what she's doing, but she's smiling real nice at me. She's got pretty eyes.

'Now, what about a nice mince pie, Billy?'